Christmas
HELLHOUND

Christmas
HELLHOUND

ZOE CHANT

Christmas Hellhound
© 2018 Zoe Chant

www.zoechant.com

CHAPTER ONE

Caine

DECEMBER 20
(CHRISTMAS EVE EVE EVE EVE EVE)

Caine was having the dream again.

He ran as fast as he could, but there was no escaping the monster. Everywhere he fled, every alleyway he sprinted down, every dark corner he hid in, the creature found him.

At last his strength gave out. He collapsed, bloodying his knees and hands on the rough ground, exhaustion roaring through him.

Everything was dark. The only sound was the rush of blood in his ears and his gasping breaths. Nothing else.

Nothing else.

Hope flared inside him, pale and delicate like the first blossoms of spring, and then the monster opened its eyes.

His eyes.

Caine burst awake, a scream echoing in his ears. One leg

kicked out, hitting something that fell over with a crash, and for a moment he couldn't remember where he was. Nothing was familiar: not the bedsheets tangled around him, not the smell of the air, not the silence. There were no traffic noises filtering in from outside, no distant or not-so-distant sirens blaring. No sounds of people at all.

One thing was still the same. Caine closed his eyes, turning his vision inwards to the deepest shadows of his soul. There it was. The dangerous monster that lived inside him.

Caine sat up wearily, getting his bearings. His hearing still seemed strangely muffled, and as he blinked and looked out the French doors at the end of his bed, he realized why. The world outside was blanketed in a thick layer of snow.

The last piece of the puzzle clicked into place. Caine remembered where he was.

Exactly where I need to be. He let out a ragged breath.

No wonder he couldn't hear any sign of human life. He was in the middle of nowhere, or more accurately, in a rented vacation cottage nestled among snow-covered trees about an hour's drive from the mountain town of Pine Valley.

Pine Valley was one of those dinky tourist towns that came to life once a year when tourists poured in for a guaranteed white Christmas. But that wasn't what had brought Caine here, five days before Christmas.

Caine grimaced. Once, he'd looked forward to Christmas. The songs, the food, the bright lights and festivities in the middle of the dark, cold winter had made the holiday magical when he was a kid. Even as an adult, the holiday had been a chance for reflection.

Now, it was a bitter reminder of the hell his life had become.

Last Christmas, Caine had discovered that magic was real. And that real magic wasn't flying reindeer and a fat man coming down the chimney to deliver presents. It was being attacked by a giant black wolf with burning eyes, and waking up the next morning with a monster living inside your soul.

A *hellhound*.

As though it had heard Caine's thoughts, the monster opened its eyes.

Caine tensed.

It was always there, lurking inside him. He could see it when he closed his eyes, smoke pouring from its jaws, and eyes that burned like twin gates to Hell itself. But he never knew what might set it off and make it try to claw its way out. And when that happened...

The nightmare was fresh enough in his mind that he couldn't stop the memory from rushing up.

His best friend Angus Parker's face changing from shock to fear as Caine transformed and attacked him.

As though it thought the memory was real, and Angus was there in the room with him, Caine's hellhound snarled. Sparks flew from its eyes. Its anger was like thunder smashing against the inside of Caine's skull.

Caine barely had time to prepare before it surged forward, trying to take form. Smoke twisted at the edges of his vision. Pain lanced through his body as the hellhound tried to take over.

No! Caine clutched his head in his hands, trying desperately to concentrate through the pain. He imagined a cage of unbreakable steel bars forming around the monster, shrinking, forcing it back to the deepest part of his soul.

The hellhound fought back. It bit and scratched at the cage, hurling itself against it until lights burst behind Caine's eyes.

He swore, pouring all his energy and concentration into the

cage, and at last the monster retreated. Caine watched it until it was so deep in the shadows that all he could see was the burning red of its eyes.

"Good," he muttered hoarsely. "And stay there. I won't let you hurt anyone else."

At least I have something to show for the last year, he thought. *Twelve-month progress review, Caine Guinness: subject has shown great improvement in controlling unacceptable outbursts. Key goals for the next period include...*

A sensation like fire crackling behind his eyes made him cut the thought off. The monster was chained, but it was still awake. And listening. He couldn't risk letting it know the true reason he was here in Pine Valley.

To destroy it.

It's been a year since I turned into a hellhound and lost everything good in my life. My job, my home, and my relationship with my best friend. But now I've got a chance at fixing things.

Who knows. Maybe, once all this is over, I'll get up the nerve to call Angus again.

Caine stretched. He'd arrived in Pine Valley mid-morning after driving overnight, and by the look of the light streaming into the bedroom it was now late afternoon. Time to head into town and make some inquiries. Follow up on the rumors he'd traced back to this remote mountain town: that Pine Valley was home to a family of dragon shifters, all of whom had almost lost their dragons.

If he could find out their secret, and jump that "almost" hurdle… he'd be free.

He'd managed to get undressed before falling into bed for once. He grabbed his pants from the end of the bed and looked for his boots. They were under the bedside table he'd knocked over as he woke from his nightmare. He pulled them on, picked up his jacket and was about to look for a shirt when a chill breeze whispered across his bare shoulders.

He tensed, scanning the room for its source. He couldn't hear an AC unit. All the doors and windows should have been shut tight, so there shouldn't be any drafts, unless—

The ice that crackled up Caine's spine when he saw that the balcony door was open had nothing to do with the breeze.

His mouth went dry. *I never opened that door.*

When I woke up just now, I didn't know if it was the monster's screams that woke me, or...

Or someone else.

The balcony door swung further open. Just an inch. But this time, the sliver of wind brought something else with it: the sound of dogs barking.

All the hairs on the back of Caine's neck stood on end. Inside him, the monster pricked up its ears.

Think sensibly, Caine ordered himself, reinforcing the psychic cage around the monster before it could try to escape. *You're half a continent away from where the hellhounds attacked you. It can't be them.*

His pulse thundered in his ears. *It's probably just dogs. This is a rural area. Rural places have dogs, ordinary dogs—*

Then a woman's shriek cut through the air.

Caine's feet hit snow before he even realized he'd jumped out the French doors and off the balcony. Where had the scream come from? He had to—

The woman shouted again and Caine started to run.

His mind was screaming. *Wild dogs. Wolves.*

Or worse.

Snow crunched under his boots. Icy wind whipped the heat

from his skin. He ran without seeing where he was going, every atom of his body straining towards the woman's voice.

The barking was getting louder. He was close. But, God, he didn't know what he was going to do if this was what he feared it was.

His nightmare, come to life. Again.

The woman shouted again. Caine's blood was pounding too hard in his ears for him to make out the words as he ran into a stand of pine trees. The trees were frozen, their boughs heavy with snow, but Caine moved between them like a ghost.

The scent of pine filled his nose, and the clean frozen smell of the snow and ice, and then the texture of the wind changed and his senses were full of *dog*.

Heart thundering, Caine burst out from under the trees.

"I'm trying to save you, you little bastards! Stop licking me! Argh! Get off!"

Caine froze. Whatever he'd expected, it wasn't this.

The pines opened out into a clearing piled high with drifts of snow. On the other side, a brightly-painted sleigh was upended in one of the drifts. For a moment, Caine's head spun. It looked for all the world like Santa's sleigh had crash-landed in the forest.

No reindeer, though, flying or otherwise. Instead, a half-dozen fluffy grey-and-white dogs clustered around the bottom of the sleigh, their leads disappearing into the snow drift.

And the shouting woman was in the middle of it all, laughing and yelling.

Relief washed over Caine like sunrise lighting up the horizon. She wasn't hurt. She wasn't in any danger. The barking dogs were just ordinary dogs, not...

He wrenched his mind away from the memory and sighed, his breath pluming out in front of him in the chill air.

It was just the nightmare getting its claws into me again. Not real. Not this time.

The woman was bundled up against the cold in a heavy, hooded jacket and dark glasses to protect against the late-afternoon sun bouncing off the snow. All that was visible of her face was a flash of brown skin and a smile as wide as the sky.

The dogs were falling over each other in their attempts to jump up on her, but her shouts weren't afraid, just annoyed. And relieved. And...

Caine breathed in. There was another scent on the air, almost hidden under the thick smell of *dog*. Something fresh and green and delicate but with a punch like hard liquor. His head spun.

"Yes, yes, I'm happy to see you too," the woman shouted, and Caine's heart leapt. "No, that's enough. Sit! All of you!"

Caine's legs gave out. He collapsed into a low-hanging branch. The branch cracked, sending snow sheeting down onto him, and the woman looked up.

The sky-wide grin dropped off her face. She pushed her sunglasses and hood off her face with one gloved hand, and Caine went completely still.

She was gorgeous. Her cheeks were covered in a wild explosion of freckles a few shades darker than her skin, and a curl of dark hair sprang out from under the woolen hat she had on under the hood. Her eyes were like rich honey, huge and intelligent and fiercely alive.

She was...

She was taking off her sunglasses because she didn't need them anymore. The snow was turning orange and red, reflecting a sunset that burned across the sky behind her like hellfire.

One of the sled dogs began to howl. One by one, the others joined in.

And deep in the darkest part of Caine's soul, his demon opened its burning eyes and looked at her.

Yes! it cried, smoke pouring from its jaws.

Caine choked out a curse and threw himself backwards. The demon had *spoken*. It had never done that before, just growled and snapped. And now its voice rang like a bell in his head.

Yes, yes! it howled. *Her! There!*

Caine's heart stopped. The monster's excitement was like fire in his veins. It had never reacted like this to anyone.

I have to get out of here. Ice crackled down his spine, fighting the demon's fiery energy. *What have I done? I ran out here to help but the only danger out here is* me.

He stood up.

I have to run. I can't let it—

"Hey! Stop right there!"

Caine's legs locked in place. The woman wasn't staring at him with wide-eyed confusion anymore—she was frowning. *Glaring.* If looks could kill, he'd be a smoking hole in the ground.

The woman jabbed one gloved finger at him. "I've got you now, asshole! Don't even think about trying to run away!"

Her voice cut through him like a red-hot knife. She was struggling through the snow and tangled-up dog team. Caine hoped for a moment that they would hold her in place, but there was no stopping her. She strode forward like an avenging angel.

She must know what I am. Caine's blood ran cold. Nothing else could explain the expression of pure, undiluted anger in her eyes.

"Wait!" he called out. The woman's eyes snapped up to meet his. "Don't come any—"

His voice broke off as darkness crackled through his veins. His demon rose up inside him, fire and shadow and smoke and *danger*, its sheer glee sending alarms blaring in Caine's mind.

She was ten feet away. Eight. Six. And his feet still wouldn't move. He was frozen in place, helpless to stop this strange, angry woman from storming into his demon's path.

I should never have come here. This was a mistake.

He could barely hear himself think over the creature's excited cries.

She's here! She sees us!

I have to stop this somehow. Please, God, don't let it hurt her.

Hurt her?

The demon turned its full attention on Caine. His breath stuttered. He'd fought his demon before, shown it his anger, his fury and rage at having his life ripped away from him—but he'd never let it feel his fear.

The woman grabbed his arm. Inside him, his demon twisted in on itself, its knife-like fangs bared. Pain and confusion poured from it, as thick and choking as the smoke it breathed. Then it leapt forward, and Caine's eyes burned as it looked out of them.

"Got you!" the woman cried triumphantly.

Caine's vision cleared. He stared into the woman's wide, honey-brown eyes.

And his demon disappeared.

CHAPTER TWO

Meaghan

Meaghan swayed on her feet. The man's eyes were on fire. And there was something behind them, something that pulsed through her like a wave of heat off a bonfire.

It felt... happy.

I'm losing it, she decided. *But there's one thing I'm damned sure of.*

I've spent all day driving around the mountain looking for those poor dogs and that ridiculous Santa sleigh. I'm tired, and hungry, and sore.

But the dogs are okay. The Santa sleigh isn't in pieces.

And not only is this guy the only person I've seen in miles, he turns up right next to the stolen sleigh and dog team?

He must be one of the assholes who took them.

"This is my lucky day," she muttered, tightening her grip on the man's arm.

"Mine too," he breathed, in a voice like caramel sauce.

Meaghan's eyebrows snapped together. "What?" she burst out, and a guilty expression flitted across his face. She took a step closer to him "Don't even think about running away! And—*argh*!"

Meaghan yelled as a crust of snow collapsed under her feet.

She struggled to catch her balance without letting go of the man. His foot slipped, too, and they half-stumbled together. Panting, Meaghan straightened up.

And found herself glaring straight at the man's... collarbones?

She shook her head. That couldn't be right. *No one* was that much taller than her. And hadn't she been looking straight into his eyes before?

His burning bonfire eyes with that wild surge of joy behind them.

She shook herself. They were wallowing in a snow-drift, that was the problem. She needed to get them both onto solid ground, so she could look into his eyes again.

No, so you can make sure he doesn't get away. What are you thinking?

The snow wasn't as deep beneath the trees. Meaghan tightened her grip on the man's arm—his bare, muscular arm—and clambered up the slight slope until she and the man were eye to...

...lips.

Really nice lips. Really, unacceptably nice and soft-looking lips, surrounded by a scruff of dark stubble.

Meaghan gritted her teeth and looked up—*up!*—into the man's eyes. They weren't burning, of course, because she'd been imagining that. Instead, they were a startling blue, like the evening sky just after sunset.

He stared back, his eyebrows furrowing sexily, and her heart sank.

Trust this to happen to you. You spend two months chasing down the assholes who've been terrorizing Pine Valley, and as soon as you manage to hunt one down, you get a freaking crush on him? Wow. Congrats, girl, this is officially the stupidest thing you have ever done.

She'd arrived at work at the Puppy Express that morning to find her coworker Olive Lockey—Olly—in tears. A couple of assholes had turned up before opening, broken into the kennels and stolen six of the sled dogs that the Puppy Express used for their Christmas Wonderland sleigh rides, as well as the Santa sleigh they'd been fixing up for the Christmas parade.

Any other time, Meaghan might have thought it was just a couple of drunk bros playing a prank. She would have gone after them regardless—no way she was letting anyone endanger the sweet doofus dogs she worked with—but this wasn't the first "prank gone wrong" that had hit Pine Valley in the last few months.

And Meaghan knew that if anyone was going to take her suspicions seriously, she was going to need some evidence.

She just wasn't expecting the evidence she found to be so hot.

Or so half-naked.

"I'm not going to run away," the man said. "In fact, I don't think I can." His voice caught slightly at the end of the sentence and Meaghan's stomach lurched.

She looked at him again. Properly this time.

He was wearing a jacket, but it was half-unzipped over his bare chest. No shirt. His pants were sweatpants, barely better than bare legs on a winter's day in the mountains, let alone when the sun was down. The laces on one of his boots were only half-tied.

Once she got past how incredibly blue his eyes were, it was impossible to miss the deep shadows around them. And the slight tremor that shook his body with every breath.

Meaghan swore under her breath. "Some friends you have, leaving you out here like this."

"Friends?" The man sounded surprised. *Genuinely* surprised. For the first time, Meaghan felt a hint of doubt.

She opened her mouth. The words *You know, your friends who helped you steal the dogs* were on the tip of her tongue when the surprise on the guy's face flickered into an expression of anxious but unmistakable guilt.

"You look like you're about to pass out," she said instead, and it wasn't difficult to make her concern sound genuine, because she was genuinely concerned that if the guy fell into some sort of hypothermic coma, she'd never get the answers she wanted. "Come on, let's—damn it, Loony, what?"

Loony—so called because she had a sort-of moon-shaped white splodge over half her face and levels of irrepressible idiocy only matched by her littermate Parkour—had somehow managed to wrangle herself out of her harness and was snorfling urgently at Meaghan's legs.

"I know you're missing your dinner, babe, but— oh *shit."* Meaghan looked past Loony to the other dogs and the upturned sleigh.

Loony wasn't snorfling for treats. She was the dog equivalent of the kid going *Mom Mom Mom* **look he's doing something** *ba-a-a-a-ad!*

"Parkour! Get off of there!"

Meaghan reluctantly let go of the man's arm. Parkour—who was just as patchwork-colored and at least three times as stupid as his littermate Loony—was scrambling up the side of the Santa sleigh.

The Santa sleigh that was upended in the snow drift.

The Santa sleigh that was upended *very precariously* in the snow drift, with all the sled dogs except Loony and Parkour tied together in its shadow. The shadow that, as Parkour clambered up the side of the upturned sled, was starting to wobble...

"Parkour, no! Down!"

Meaghan raced back across the clearing. *Let the dog-napper try to run. If that sleigh falls down and hurts any of the dogs, hypothermia is going to be the least of his worries.*

"Heel!" she screamed as the sleigh toppled slowly down.

The dogs tried to obey. The four dogs standing under the sleigh surged toward her, dragging Parkour down by his harness. He yelped and scrabbled against the sleigh as his lead tangled around one of the runners.

Meaghan had just made it into the sleigh's shadow as it gave an enormous groan and began to topple down. Loony wove herself between Meaghan's legs as she tried to back up.

"Look out!"

A pale-man-colored flash whipped past her. Meaghan barely had time to realize she'd come within an inch of being brained by the falling sleigh before it was crashing into the snow six feet away.

Loony nudged against her legs again and Meaghan sank down to her knees. The rest of the dogs trotted up, tails wagging. Meaghan unclipped them from their tangled leads. They were all covered in snow. Some of them were wriggling with excitement, but skinny Chubbs was shaking with exhaustion. Meaghan ruffled his ears as he tried to climb into her lap.

"Come on puppies, let me see—oh, you're all fine, you're all wonderful. *Good* dogs. You're all so good. Even you, Parkour, you massive idiot."

She didn't cry. Hours and hours of freaking out about what the assholes who'd terrified her coworker and stolen the dogs might do to them, and following sled tracks through paths that weren't even paths, just gaps in the forest, and it was all okay, they were all fine and not run past the point of exhaustion and not squished under the stupid Santa parade sleigh. Everything was fine. There was no reason for her to cry.

So she buried her face in Chubbs' fluffy shoulder and waited for her chest to stop heaving.

"Are you all right?"

Meaghan raised her head.

The guy was *still there*. He hadn't taken advantage of her being distracted to run away—not that he would have gotten far, half-naked in the frozen wilderness.

And then she would have had to chase him down. Again. Bad enough that she was probably going to have to check him in at the doctor's clinic before tossing him in the lockup and throwing away the key.

Forget crying. She was still mad.

"Oh I am *better* than fine." Meaghan stood up and brushed clumps of snow off her knees. *And your bad day is only just getting started.* The man looked dazed. "What's your name?"

"Caine. Caine Guinness."

"Right." *Now I know what to have engraved on your gravestone,* she added silently.

"And..." Caine licked his lower lip. Meaghan clenched her fists, reminding herself that this guy was an asshole of the highest order and she was *not* attracted to him. "You are...?"

Not letting myself get distracted by your face. Or chest. Or the fact that you just saved me from being splatted when you could have been making your getaway.

Asshole.

She narrowed her eyes. The guy—Caine—was acting all meek and innocent now, but how long was that going to last? She needed to get him back to town. And if he'd leapt to her aid once...

Meaghan let herself fall backwards, arms windmilling dramatically. Caine jumped into action. He moved through the knee-deep snow as though it was nothing and caught her before she hit the ground.

This is just to get him to the truck, Meaghan told herself firmly, her eyes two inches from Caine's carved-marble chest.

"Are you all right?"

Meaghan faked a gasp of pain. "I stepped in a hole—twisted my ankle. Can you help me get back to my truck?"

"I..." Caine hesitated, and the frustration and worry that had been gnawing at Meaghan since Halloween flared.

"Get me to my truck!"

So much for pretending to be a damsel in distress. But it worked. Caine lifted her up—like she weighed nothing, holy shit, she might not be a damsel but he was doing a damn good job of pretending to be Prince Charming—and carried her to her truck.

Meaghan had driven as far off-road as she dared, following the sound of dogs barking. Her rust-bucket truck had four-wheel drive... technically. Some days it felt more like one-wheel drive.

But it had made it up the mountain. She was sure it would make it down again.

She patted her phone in her jacket pocket. When she'd originally come haring after the stolen dogs, she'd figured she would call her boss when she found them and get him to drive up with the dog truck. But that was before she had a near-hypothermic dog-napper on her hands.

Meaghan narrowed her eyes. The dogs would be happy enough in the back. And as for Caine...

"Help me get the dogs in?" she said casually.

Caine nodded and set her down. She grabbed a blanket from the trunk and thrust it at him.

"You'd better take that. Wrap yourself up. And—here. Crush these up and hold onto them, they'll keep your hands warm."

Meaghan passed him a handful of the self-heating handwarmers Olly was always slipping into her pockets.

"Thanks," he said, awkwardly trying to wrap the blanket around himself and take the handwarmers at the same time.

Don't thank me, thank the woman you left freaked out and crying after you stole the sleigh! Meaghan bit the inside of her cheek to stop herself yelling at him.

The truck's back door stuck a bit, but she jiggled it open. The dogs were clustered around her and Caine's legs, waiting for her orders.

"Up!" she chirped. Caine jerked, and the dogs jumped in, each finding somewhere to snuggle in on the cracked vinyl seats.

Chubbs tried to jump up last of all, but missed his footing and fell back, feet scrabbling. Caine leaned over and lifted him in, apparently without thinking.

He reached into the back of the truck to scratch Chubbs behind the ears and looked at Meaghan over his shoulder. The truck's inside light backlit him, putting his face in shadow.

"I came to Pine Valley expecting—I don't know what. Not this."

Was that a smile, or a rueful grimace? Meaghan felt herself softening despite herself. There was something strangely... compelling about Caine. God knew she had more than enough reasons to hate every inch of him, but every time he glanced at her, or smiled—he was smiling now, wasn't he?—it took her off guard.

The shadow at one corner of his mouth deepened. "You knew what I was the moment you saw me, and—"

Right. Good feelings gone.

"You're right," Meaghan snarled. "Thanks for reminding me!"

She shoved him as hard as she could into the back of the truck and slammed the door shut. Caine yelled in surprise but Meaghan ignored him as she ran to the driver's seat and started the engine.

"I know exactly what you are. And what you've been doing. And you might be—" Handsome, and charming, and distractingly half-naked... "—*ugh*. You've been a pain in my side for two months, but that ends now! I'm not going to let you ruin Christmas!"

CHAPTER THREE

Caine

Ruin Christmas?

The truck lurched into reverse and Caine slid face-first into a pile of dogs.

What the hell just happened?

A damp nose whuffled in Caine's ear. He pushed himself up and the dogs made space for him on the battered-looking seats.

The woman was hunched over the wheel. She glanced at him in the rear-view mirror just long enough for her eyebrows to clang together in a ferocious glare, then swung the truck around and kept her eyes firmly forward.

He cleared his throat. "Excuse me," he said, pitching his voice to cut through the grumbling engine. "If you're kidnapping me, I feel like I should at least know why."

"You know what you did!"

"Can I at least know your name—"

"Stop asking questions!"

Caine's mouth snapped shut. He sighed and sat back. One of the dogs noodled its way onto his lap and he petted it absently.

Clearly, this woman had him mixed up with someone else.

Caine opened his mouth to explain that he hadn't been in town long enough to cause any trouble—and then shut it again.

His head was spinning. He didn't know what was going on, or who this woman was or who she thought *he* was—but one thing he knew without a doubt.

His demon was gone.

He closed his eyes, hunting deep in the shadows of his soul. There was nothing there. For the first time in twelve months, he was alone in his own head.

Caine breathed in. The truck smelled of diesel and wet dog—and that was it. No underlay of scents that should have been impossible for him to smell, let alone identify. He heard the truck's engine and the soft grumbles and whines of the dogs piled up around him. Nothing else. The headlights lit up the road in front of them, and *he couldn't see into the shadows.*

He was human again.

Caine slumped backwards. Two more dogs took the opportunity to wriggle up onto his lap and stomach.

Human. And all it had taken was being kidnapped by a strange, gorgeous, shouty woman.

He could live with that.

The road wound through snow-covered pine trees. Caine didn't recognize the route. He'd deliberately avoided going through town on his way into the mountains. From everything he'd heard, Pine Valley was like the North Pole on steroids during the holiday season. He hadn't wanted to risk any of the locals getting on his hellhound's bad side—and he'd wanted to avoid the fact that it was almost Christmas as long as possible.

Until now. Now, maybe he would have a happy Christmas after all.

CHAPTER FOUR

Meaghan

The road back to the Puppy Express was mostly potholes. She tried to avoid them, but it was impossible to miss them all.

Every time one of Meaghan's wheels hit one, her stomach lurched and her brain followed it down—*This has to work, what if it doesn't, you don't even know why everyone's been behaving so weird but what if you just make it worse...*

Good thing about potholes, though, if you hit them hard enough you just went bouncing up the other side again.

This will *work. And I might not know what's made everyone act so freaking weird ever since I suggested that what's been going on might be more than just coincidence...*

...But I am going to fix it.

The Puppy Express building appeared through a gap in the trees. Meaghan hauled the truck around the last corner and parked in the middle of the empty lot in front of the building.

Her fingers tightened on the wheel. The Puppy Express "stationhouse" was built to look like a frontier-style log cabin, but sized for a giant. Its windows were painted red and the snow piled up on the windowpanes and roof was real enough—despite its rustic look, the Express building was snugly insulated, so not even a hint of the cozy heat from the open fireplace inside leaked out to melt the snow.

Warm golden light poured out the windows, green and red fairy lights sparkled along the eaves, and a huge sign proclaiming *Home of the Puppy Express* hung over the entranceway.

Just below it, someone with his own special sense of humor—Meaghan's boss, Bob—had hung another series of signs that read: *Merry Christmas Eve Eve Eve Eve Eve.*

It was all very cheerful and festive and Christmassy, except for the fact that it was five days before Christmas and the only vehicle in the parking lot was Meaghan's truck.

The Puppy Express was one of Pine Valley's most popular tourist attractions during the holiday season. Visitors could take rides on sleds or Christmas-decorated sleighs pulled by adorable dogs along snowy routes that wound around the mountain. At special stops, they could get out, stretch their legs, maybe have a picnic, and *definitely* write a Christmas card to their loved ones and pop it in one of the special mail boxes.

Everything about it was one hundred per cent ridiculously cute, right down to the branded sweaters in the gift shop. Meaghan had been thrilled to get a job there when she arrived in town six months before. Hanging out with dogs all the time? What could be better?

If there were enough tourists to make it worth opening up every day, she thoughts grimly. Bob had started wincing every time he looked at the desk where he sat to do the weekly accounts. All those "pranks" and "accidents" the last few months had put visitor numbers into freefall.

Someone must have heard Meaghan's truck roaring up the drive. A figure appeared at one of the windows. Meaghan recognized it as Olly by the way she stayed lurking halfway behind the windowsill. Olly might be chill most of the time, but she had some weird hang-ups around getting the jump on people before they saw her.

Like you have some weird hang-ups around bulldozing your way into other people's business.

Meaghan grinned. It was a surprise she and Olly got on as well as they did, but somehow, being opposites suited their friendship nicely.

She jumped out of the truck and strode around to the back doors, rolling her shoulders to ease all the knots and tension that had built up during her day of hunting for the stolen dogs.

"Here we are!" she called out, tapping on the side of the truck. "Who's happy to be home, huh, doofuses?"

The dogs were already barking with excitement. It was already dark, and to them, dark plus home equaled dinnertime.

I hope my guest isn't getting too *trampled,* Meaghan thought piously. Then: *Nah. That's a lie. Trample him to pieces, dogs!*

The front door of the Puppy Express stationhouse burst open and Meaghan's boss, Bob Lockey, jogged down the steps.

"That you, Meaghan? Thank Christ. The last thing we need is you disappearing on us as well. Olly told me some story about you going after the pricks who ran off without paying, but it's all under control, Officer Gilles is here and..."

Meaghan leaned back against the truck's back door with a grin, and Bob's eyes narrowed.

"...Meaghan, what have you done?"

Bob Lockey was Olly's uncle. He was in his mid-fifties, with light brown skin and hair so white-blond that even locals sometimes offered him a senior's discount if they weren't paying too much attention to who they were serving. Add the curly beard he'd been cultivating since Meaghan moved into Pine Valley six months ago and it was no surprise he'd been picked to play Santa Claus in the town's Christmas parade and fair.

Right now, he was looking like a very suspicious Santa Claus.

Jackson Gilles, the town's trainee police officer, trotted down the stairs behind Bob. When he caught sight of Meaghan, he heaved a dramatic sigh and slowed from a trot to a saunter. Meaghan snorted.

Jackson had popped up every time she'd gone looking into one of the "pranks" or "accidents" that had happened in Pine Valley over the last few months. He'd always seemed more interested in keeping her away than listening to her suspicions about how they were all connected.

I might be a thorn in your side but at least I'm getting things done.

There was no sign of Olly, but that didn't worry Meaghan. Frankly, she'd be more concerned if Olly was standing front and center instead of keeping watch from the sidelines.

"Causing trouble, Megs?" Jackson called out.

"Why? You seen any?" she shot back. Bob was still peering at her suspiciously. She nodded at him, and couldn't stop a triumphant grin from spreading across her face. "Olly told you right, boss, I've been out looking for the dogs. And I found them. *And* one of the assholes who stole them."

Bob paled behind his beard. "You *what?*"

Behind him, Jackson ran his fingers through his dark hair. "Christ, Megs, why would you do that?"

Meaghan was flabbergasted by their reactions. They didn't look just surprised by what she'd done, they looked *scared.* She threw her arms up.

"Why? *Why?* So that maybe you would listen to me about what's happening right under your noses! All the pranks and accidents and, and the toy store burning down aren't *coincidences*! Someone is trying to ruin Christmas in Pine Valley, and I've finally tracked them down!"

Bob swore under his breath. His cheeks were as white as his beard. "Meaghan, don't tell me you've brought one of them—"

She yanked on the door. It didn't open. She hauled on the handle again. "Damn it, come *on*, you pile of junk," she muttered as Jackson grabbed her arm.

"That's not a good idea, Megs," he said, trying to pull her away. "You shouldn't have gone out there."

Meaghan stood her ground. "What are you on about? At least I'm doing something! Didn't you see how upset Olly was, or don't you care?"

Jackson jerked back as though she'd slapped him, and Meaghan bit her lip. That had been too far. She knew Jackson had a thing for Olly.

She yanked on the door again and it popped open.

"There!" she announced, standing to one side and flourishing an angry arm at Caine, who was lounging—*lounging!*—among the dogs.

Chubbs was snuggled on his lap.

Traitor, Meaghan grumbled silently.

Caine looked the picture of innocence. She glared at his chest and gulped. Even covered with dog hair and with Chubbs' nose wedged under his armpit, he was... *ugh.*

Then he licked his lips which, frankly, wasn't a fair move.

Jackson had let go of her arm as she opened the door, and now she rounded on him.

"I know you think I'm crazy, and you don't think everything that's happened is connected, but I'm telling you, it *is*. Olly said three guys came in here and stole the dogs, and this is one of them. Ask him about the fire at Mr. Bell's store—and the other weird stuff that's been happening!"

Someone tapped on Meaghan's shoulder.

She jumped and spun around. "Olly! I thought you were still inside. How are you? Are you okay?"

Meaghan grabbed her friend's arm, and Olly gave her a small smile.

Olly was a few years younger than Meaghan. Her pale hazel eyes were still as wide as they'd been when Meaghan found her just after Caine and his asshole friends had stolen the dogs, but she didn't look as tense.

In fact, Meaghan thought she could detect a hint of amusement in her expression.

"I'm not bad," Olly reassured her. "But I'm sorry, Meaghan, the guy in your truck is *not* one of the assholes we're after."

Meaghan froze. "What?" She searched Olly's face for any clue that this was a joke. "Are you sure?"

"I think I remember what the three guys who broke in here in front of me looked like," Olly retorted. She leaned around Meaghan and peered into the truck, her eyes narrowing as though she were inspecting Caine carefully. "And they were definitely not like him."

Jackson let out a huff of relief. "Thank God for that." He turned away, kicking at the snow, and Meaghan thought she heard him say something like, *Not like I could have done much if he was.*

She frowned. What was he talking about? He was the deputy sheriff. He was the only one in town with the authority *to* do anything!

If Caine had been one of the criminals.

Which…

Meaghan spun around and stared directly into Caine's eyes for the first time since she'd shoved him in the back of her truck.

Oh my God. Have I just made the biggest mistake in my entire life?

Was Caine a smoking hot, helpful and caring... not-dog-napper?

"No, he definitely is," she said out loud, her head swimming. "Because... he was... I mean, he was *right there*... you tell them!"

She turned back to Caine, who held his hands palm-up. Loony licked one of them, as though she thought he was holding up an invisible treat.

"I'm afraid she's right," he said. "I've never met any of these people before. I'm afraid I still don't know exactly what's going on, but whatever happened here, I—" A relieved smile spread across his face. "I had nothing to do with it."

"What? But..."

Meaghan's voice sputtered out, like her truck when it was low on gas.

Caine was still sitting meekly in the middle of the pile of dogs. In the back of her truck. Where she'd pushed him in.

Where she'd... kidnapped... him?

The burning center of Meaghan's wildfire anger fell in on itself. Except for the bit of it that migrated to her cheeks.

"Are you sure?" Meaghan took a leap of what she hoped was faith but was probably actually total stupidity.

"Positive. I only arrived in town this morning."

"But... Why were you out in the woods then?"

"Ah," said Caine. "I'm staying at a ski cottage. I woke up, heard you shouting, and wanted to see if I could..."

"...help," Meaghan completed for him wanly.

Behind her there was the distinct sound of someone not laughing. Possibly several someones.

"I—then why did—why didn't you say anything?"

"I—"

"Why did you let me throw you in the truck?" Her voice was getting higher.

"Maybe if you let him get a word in, he'd tell you," Jackson drawled.

Meaghan's throat went tight. Jackson was just being an ass, but—she'd spent the last six months building a life in Pine Valley, and the last two months had shaken the foundations of everything she thought she'd achieved here. She knew she could go too far sometimes, and maybe this was it. Already.

She'd never managed to burn all her bridges in half a year before.

Her throat was so tight her breath made a rasping noise. She looked away from Caine but as she did his eyes flashed. For a moment they didn't look blue—they looked *dark*, with a shimmer of something like smoke in their depths.

Meaghan stared, but his eyes were blue again. She shook herself. Of course they were blue. They'd *always* been blue.

Except for that one moment back in the clearing, when she'd lost her mind.

Meaghan swayed and beside her, Olly tensed. And burst out laughing.

She got hold of herself a second later, and clapped one hand over her mouth, her shoulders shaking.

Meaghan stared at her. "What now?"

"Nothing!" Olly squeaked from behind her hand.

"Are you *sure* you're okay?" Meaghan frowned. "Do you need to go sit down?"

She's more freaked out than I thought.

Meaghan had arrived at work only a few minutes after the dog-nappers had left. Olly had been cowering behind the

28

customer service desk in the gift shop, looking as though she'd seen a ghost. The assholes hadn't hurt her, or taken anything except the dogs and sleigh, but they'd rattled Olly more than Meaghan had thought possible.

Meaghan had wavered between staying with her and chasing after the dogs, but when Olly had reassured her that Bob was only a few minutes away, Meaghan had…

Left her alone to start my career as a kidnapper. I'm the worst friend ever.

Jackson strode over and reached out one hand to *almost* touch Olly's shoulder.

"Megs is right," he murmured. Meaghan resisted the urge to stare. Those were three words she'd never expected out of his mouth. He hovered protectively at Olly's shoulder. "I know, I know, you said you're fine, but…"

Please let this be one good thing to come out of me screwing all this up, Meaghan begged silently. *Please let Jackson finally admit to Olly that he's been crushing on her all the time I've known them, and her on him, too…*

Olly waved them both away. "This is *so good,*" she squeaked through her giggles. Meaghan and Jackson exchanged a look.

Well. That was both super un-reassuring and super confusing. She's totally lost it.

"Okay, Olly, let's go inside…"

"Hold up a moment, Meaghan." Bob cleared his throat and Meaghan waited for him to continue, but he just stared into the middle distance and hrmm'd. Stared a bit longer. Chuckled.

Meaghan sighed. Bob was always going off into a daydream like this. Olly, too. Sometimes she felt like she was the only person at the Puppy Express who lived full-time in the real world.

She tried to catch Jackson's eye again, but he was glaring at the ground.

Caine groaned and clutched his head, and she jumped to high alert.

"Oh shit. Are you all right?" *Did he hit his head when I shoved him in there? Did I give him a concussion on top of everything else?*

"It's nothing. A headache. I—" Caine paused, but this time it wasn't Meaghan interrupting him, it was Parkour licking his chin.

Meaghan's stomach twisted. No wonder the dogs liked him. He wasn't some criminal vandal, he was just... just a regular guy. Who she'd kidnapped.

"I'm so sorry about all of this," she muttered. "I wish you'd said something."

Caine fended Parkour off with a pet. "Well, you did seem to know what you were doing." One corner of his mouth hooked up in a half-smile that caught Meaghan's heart, and then he winced again. "So, what's the plan now?"

The wince made guilt twist inside her, but that flash of smile somehow gave her the confidence to rally. She could wallow in embarrassment and guilt, or she could pick herself up and find some way to make this right.

Meaghan straightened her shoulders. *No wallowing. Go for it. All-or-nothing. What's the worst that can happen?*

Except for you getting fired five days before Christmas.

Okay. All-or-nothing. But no crazy.

"What's the plan? This is. Someone's got to get you home." His eyes lit up and Meaghan sucked in her bottom lip in embarrassment. *Yeah, I bet you can't wait to get home after I pulled you into all this.* "And—and—" *Don't say save Christmas.* "—and feed the dogs and get them settled in—" *Don't mention your conspiracy theory.* "—and go and get the sleigh... I can do that, I know where it is and if we hitch the trailer to my truck—"

30

"No!" Bob half-shouted, then smoothed down his beard and cleared his throat. He nodded at Olly, who dragged Jackson's shoulder down to whisper something in his ear. "I don't think that's a good idea, Meaghan. You shouldn't have gone out there on your own in the first place. What if you did bump into the thieves?"

Meaghan snorted. "I'm not scared of a couple of drunk assholes."

Bob groaned and rubbed his face. "Sometimes, what you don't know *can* hurt you. All right, all right, Olly, I'm getting there," he added, even though Olly hadn't said anything.

He directed an interrogating look at Caine. "So what's your story, er…"

"Caine Guinness." Caine reached out of the dog box to shake Bob's hand.

"Huh. Good, good. What brings you to town, Caine?"

"Business."

"And you just drove in today, you said? That's a long drive. You must be starving." Bob clapped his hands together. "Right! Jackson, you take Olly home, and then we'll both go and fetch the sleigh. If the thieves are still out there, we'll deal with them. Meaghan, you can tell us where it is."

"I can *show* you where it is—"

"No, you can't. Someone needs to show Caine here that Pine Valley hospitality isn't just being stuffed in the back of a truck with a pile of dogs. Get him some proper clothes from the gift shop, and—"

He grinned. Olly grinned. Even Jackson grinned. Meaghan felt a sensation of oncoming doom.

"—take him to dinner."

CHAPTER FIVE

Caine

I'm free. Free, and about to spend the evening with a gorgeous woman. I'd almost given up hoping life could be this good again.

Caine felt like he was floating as he pulled on a borrowed Puppy Express-branded hat and stepped outside. The snow, the starry night sky, the way his breath puffed out in front of him in huge clouds—it was all perfect. Everything was perfect. It was five days before Christmas and he'd just received the best gift he could have asked for.

His demon was gone. Sure, there were some lingering after-effects. Ever since he'd been infected with the creature, he got a pounding headache whenever he was around other shifters. The headache had struck again when he met Meaghan's boss and the others—they must have been shifters—but that was all. No bared teeth gnawing at his soul. No darkness inside him, clawing to get out.

He was human again. And going to dinner with the most fascinating woman he'd met before or after the demon.

Merry Christmas indeed.

Snow crunched under his boots as he hurried to catch up with

Meaghan, who was trudging head-down towards her truck.

"What do you think?" He waited until he had her attention, then did a slow turn. Bob had given him free rein in the clothing section of the Puppy Express gift shop, and it was possible he'd let his newfound freedom go to his head.

Meaghan's mouth dropped open. She snapped it shut. "Aren't you cold?"

Caine looked down. He had exchanged his thin sweatpants for a pair of insulated snow pants with a holly pattern on the cuffs. They were a few inches short—nothing in the store had really fit—but his ankles were snug under thick woolen socks with candy canes on them. The snowflake-print t-shirt stretched tight across his chest completed the look.

He'd forgotten to zip up his jacket again, but...

He glanced up. Meaghan was still glaring at him. More specifically, at his chest.

"I'm fine," he said. Sure, the evening was chilly, but the sight of Meaghan's eyes sizzling warmed him up better than any jacket.

"Well, if you fall over with frostbite I'm going to feel even worse than I already do. Take these. More handwarmers. Olly's giving them out like candy. Probably because we don't have enough visitors to use them all up and they're taking up space."

She handed him another couple of handwarmers like the ones he'd forgotten to use earlier. "Crunch them up a bit and put them in your—you're not wearing gloves. Your hands are going to freeze off and it's going to be all my fault."

"No, here, see?" Caine pulled a pair of gloves out of his pocket and Meaghan's shoulders visibly relaxed. She rubbed the base of her neck.

"Okay, well, good. So. Dinner. What do you feel like? There should be one or two places open."

"Whatever you recommend."

Caine hurried ahead of Meaghan to open the driver's side door for her and found himself facing down a glare almost as ferocious as when she thought he'd stolen her dogs.

"You are *not* driving," she said. "Look, I know this whole dinner thing is to get me back for acting like a crazy person, but believe me, *you* driving *my* truck would be more of a punishment for you than for me."

Caine blinked. "I don't want to drive. I was holding the door for you."

"Oh." Meaghan's glare lost some of its ferocity. "...Thanks?"

She folded herself into the seat, avoiding Caine's eyes. Caine frowned. He might feel as though he was flying six inches above the ground, but he'd have his head in the clouds not to see that Meaghan was upset about something.

And he wanted desperately for that not to be the case.

He wedged himself into the passenger seat and caught Meaghan glancing at him.

"It's a tight fit," he said, angling his knees under the dash.

"You get used to it." Meaghan winced. "I mean, *I've* gotten used to it. I spend most of my time with the dogs, anyway, so that gives me plenty of time to stretch my legs."

"You don't think I'll have time to get used to it, too?" he teased.

"It's not that far into town," Meaghan replied, not getting his meaning. She made a frustrated "*mmf*" noise as the truck wobbled over a bump in the road, and Caine's blood ran hot.

He hadn't so much as flirted with a woman since last Christmas. And now he wanted to do a hell of a lot more than flirt.

But whatever Caine's hopes, Meaghan clearly had her mind somewhere else. Caine racked his brains for a topic of conversation that might lift the glare from her face.

"The dogs like you a lot," he settled on. "And you must like them too, going to all that effort to find them."

"Of course I like them. They're good dogs, they get on well with everyone, even... even crazy women who go around kidnapping people." She sighed. "I am so sorry about that. God, I must really be losing it."

Her scowl wasn't going anywhere. Caine was about to try again when she shook her head and tapped her palms on the steering wheel.

"I just—these last few months—no. No excuses. I'm crazy, and I jumped to conclusions, and I'm sorry for... everything."

"Don't be."

Meaghan snorted. "Trust me, you do *not* want to encourage me about this. I am one hundred percent capable of throwing myself into bad ideas without any help."

"What bad ideas, exactly?"

"Where should I start? How about moving to a new town where I don't know anyone. Getting a job at a tourist shop right before their worst year for tourist numbers in decades..." She tapped the steering wheel again. "Nope. Don't say it, girl. Keep the lid on the crazy."

Caine's instincts were pricking. Not his demon's instincts, but the ones that he'd honed in his old life as a private investigator.

Something was making Meaghan upset. Something that had driven her to save the dogs from whoever had stolen them, and to shove him in the back of her truck.

And he had a suspicion she was getting close to revealing what it was. Or letting it boil out of her, at least.

"Don't say what?" he prompted. She groaned.

"I warned you, don't encourage me..." Meaghan narrowed her eyes at him and turned her attention back to the road. "Fine. You asked for it. I think there's more to the low tourist numbers this year than just bad luck. Because numbers aren't just *low*, they're in the negatives. Even some locals are staying away from Pine Valley this Christmas."

"Why?"

Meaghan was bubbling over with frustration, but something was still stopping her. "Keep in mind this is crazy conspiracy level stuff we're talking here."

"Is that what you really think?" *How many people have told her that?*

"No. It's not." Meaghan made a face. "Fine. There's been… stuff happening. Weird stuff. Ever since Halloween."

The skin on the back of Caine's neck prickled. "You mentioned something about a toy store burning down."

"Everyone says it was an accident."

"And you don't believe them."

Caine watched Meaghan's face as she decided how to answer. She gnawed on her bottom lip, squeezed her eyes shut for a second, and groaned.

"No, I *don't* believe them. And I think it's going to get worse. I don't know how much you know about Pine Valley, but—"

"Assume I know nothing."

Meaghan took a deep breath, and then shrugged. "Okay. The hell with it. So, Pine Valley is a tourist town. Lives and dies—pay attention to that last part—on people visiting on their vacation and spending money locally. The biggest draws are Halloween, when all the trees turn fall colors, and Christmas, because, well, it's a cute little town in the mountains that gets a lot of snow."

She rolled her shoulders back. They clicked so loudly that Caine winced in sympathy… and wished he could reach out and massage them.

"Stuff started to get *weird* around Halloween. I mean, there's a limit to the number of trees that can fall down right in front of a tour bus, or how often all the streetlights can short out at the same time, right? Or people saying they were almost run off the road by some sort of freaky wild animals with scary glowing eyes? It can't all be random. They *have* to be connected."

Caine tensed. "Glowing eyes?"

Meaghan gestured angrily. "Jackson just says that all animals have glowing eyes when they get caught in headlights, but some of the people I talked to said their eyes weren't just glowing, they were on *fire*. It's got to be someone dressed up or some sort of trick, right? But no one remembers anything about what they looked like except for the eyes, and that seeing them *really* freaked them out."

"And they've been running people off the road? Chasing them?"

"No one's been hurt, thank God. But some tourists skidded into a snow drift after the driver thought he saw one of these ghost-things. And some people say they saw them on some of the Puppy Express routes, which took a chunk out of bookings. No one wants to go out on a magical sleighride and get eaten by wild animals."

"Ghosts," Caine said quietly. *Burning eyes. Spreading terror. This all sounds too familiar.*

"That's what I've been calling them. The ghost gang. Because it can't just be one person, right? And now we know it isn't, because Olly says it was three guys who broke into the Puppy Express this morning." She frowned and her voice became uncertain. "Or—not broke in exactly—it looked more like they snuck in somehow without her seeing, and then smashed things up as they broke *out*..."

37

A full-body shiver grabbed hold of Caine. *Walking through walls. Remember that?*

The night the hellhounds had attacked him, he'd run through the streets, trying to throw them off. He'd thought he'd lost them at the end of a maze of garbage-filled alleyways and abandoned lots, but then one of the monsters had walked straight through a brick wall in front of him.

He shook his head. He was jumping to conclusions. Besides, there definitely were other shifters in Pine Valley. The whole reason Caine was here was to find a dragon shifter and ask for his help. If this "ghost gang" really were like him, then wouldn't a *dragon* have dealt with them by now?

"You don't believe me." Meaghan's voice was flat.

"No, I don't—I don't *not* believe you." Caine winced. That sounded fake even to him.

"Don't worry about it. You're in good company. No one else believes there's anything weird going on, either."

"Something supernatural," Caine suggested carefully. "What you've described sounds kind of like… shapeshifters."

Meaghan laughed. "Come on. Even I wouldn't go that far. I said conspiracy theory, not aliens."

Caine relaxed. She hadn't taken the bait. *She must not know about shifters.*

Meaghan's shoulders slumped. "No supernatural stuff needed. Just me being crazy and butting in where I'm not wanted. Making bad decisions. Kidnapping innocent tourists—seriously, you must be the only visitor in town right now and look at the welcome I gave you."

"What makes you think kidnapping me was a bad decision?"

Meaghan was watching the road but at that, her eyes went wide. She pulled over and turned fully toward Caine, her expression incredulous.

"Excuse me? Why was *kidnapping you* a bad idea? Did you hit your head before I found you or—" She bit down on one knuckle and groaned. "Did you hit your head when I... pushed you into the back of my truck..."

Caine laughed. "My head's fine. And I'm completely serious. I came to Pine Valley for—business—" The lie almost stuck to the back of his tongue but he managed to spit it out. "...and instead I get a free ride to town, some stylish new clothes—"

Meaghan snorted again but this time, the corners of her mouth curved up. Caine's smile widened in response. His heartbeat sped up.

"And I get to spend the evening finding out everything you've pulled together about this ghost gang."

Meaghan stopped biting her knuckle. "You're serious. You do believe me?"

Her eyes were fixed on his. Caine felt like he was drowning in their honey-brown depths.

"Yes," he reassured her. "And I want to know more. About the ghost gang, and what they've done... and how we can stop them."

And if it means I get to spend more time with you... well, that's the cherry on top.

Meaghan's eyes flashed. She straightened her shoulders.

"I'd better get us into town before you change your mind, then," she said.

Her grin lit up Caine's heart.

*

Half an hour later, Meaghan's grin was fading, and Caine's heart was troubled.

39

The Puppy Express was just out of town, but there'd been no traffic on the roads. Even as they wound through the outskirts of Pine Valley township, the streets were eerily quiet.

"Least we'll have no trouble finding a parking spot," Meaghan muttered, turning up a wide street.

Caine frowned. "Is this the middle of town?"

"Smack bang in the center." Meaghan grimaced. "You could have gotten a room right in the square for peanuts, instead of renting way out in the woods."

"It didn't even occur to me to look at anything this central." He'd wanted the safety of solitude, not easy access to town—but that wasn't a problem now. He grinned, relief washing over him again.

"Usually everywhere in town's booked out months in advance. But this year... well. Like I said. Freaky shit is up, and bookings are down."

The brakes made a crunching sound as she parked. Caine dashed around to the driver's door to open it for her before she'd finished fighting with her seatbelt. This time, she didn't glare at him as he held the door.

At least, not as much.

And it wasn't his face she was glaring at.

Her eyes slid sideways. It was hard to tell, with her dark skin and only the light from the streetlights to see by, but Caine was almost certain she was blushing.

"Are you *seriously* not cold right now?" she muttered.

Caine looked down. His Puppy Express winter coat was still hanging open, revealing the stretch-cotton t-shirt he was wearing underneath. A smug warmth rolled through him. "Not particularly."

Meaghan grumbled something inaudible, which Caine took as

encouragement.

"Another reason why you kidnapping me wasn't a bad idea. I don't have a clue how to dress out here in the mountains. I might have frozen solid if you hadn't bundled me into the back of the truck with your dogs."

"You wouldn't have *been* outside if you hadn't heard me shouting," she retorted.

"Maybe not. I still would have heard the dogs, though. I might have gone chas—looking for them anyway, and without you, I'd be a block of ice right now."

Chasing. Hunt. Just ordinary words, but... too close. Even with his monster gone. Caine shook himself, then caught Meaghan looking at him and turned it into an exaggerated shiver. She rolled her eyes and looked away.

He'd forgotten what it was like. Being a normal person. Getting to know someone without constantly watching over his own shoulder. Messing around. Joking.

And he knew just how to spend his first Christmas as a regular human again. Helping this incredible woman uncover who'd been sabotaging the town's holiday cheer.

"Do they not have snow where you come from? No offense, but you don't strike me as the tropical island type. Not enough of a tan." Meaghan headed up the street and Caine followed her, his boots crunching on the salted sidewalk.

"Have pity on a poor city boy. I'm not used to being more than six feet from a well-heated coffee shop. I—what is *that?*"

They turned a corner at the end of the street and the night exploded in a dazzling display of golden lights. Caine blinked. Beside him, so close he could have put his arm around her, Meaghan laughed.

"How did you manage to miss it when you drove in?"

41

"I didn't come in through town. Didn't want to—" Caine licked his lips. "Uh, get caught in traffic."

"Any other Christmas, that would be smart." Meaghan sighed. "Pity. The town square is a *slightly* nicer introduction to Pine Valley than being thrown in the back of a truck."

"Oh, I wouldn't be so sure. At least the truck didn't blind me."

Meaghan looked at him like she wasn't sure if he was laughing at her or with her. For a moment Caine felt like he was on the edge of a precipice—then she snorted with laughter.

"O come all ye faithful, and gaze upon the glory of the Heartwell Christmas Tree! Well. It's more of a Christmas Forest these days."

Caine hesitated. "Did you say Heartwell?"

Meaghan stuffed her hands in her pockets and rocked back on her heels, surveying the "Christmas Forest".

"Uh-huh. Old local family. They run a trust for the town decorations and have gone *all out* this year."

Caine blinked at the scene in front of them. "I'll say."

Christmas trees of all sizes filled the square, blazing with light from strings of Christmas lights wound around and between them. The largest trees towered above the buildings, and the smallest ones barely came up to Caine's knees. It looked as though a magical forest had sprouted up in the middle of town, and the old-fashioned shop fronts that lined the square added to the fairy-tale atmosphere.

The Heartwells did this? he wondered. *A family of dragon shifters… who are really, really into tinsel?*

"What do you think?" Meaghan's eyes were sharp.

Caine considered his answer. "It's great."

Then he reconsidered. The "Christmas Forest" was an incredible feat, clearly, but there was something slightly off about it.

And not just the thought that it had been designed and paid for by a family of people who could turn into giant, fire-breathing mythological animals.

"But where is everyone?"

The town square Christmas display was magical, festive… and deserted. No small children running through the trees while their parents struggled with shopping bags. No couples wandering arm-in-arm under the lights. There was a brightly painted caravan under the largest tree that looked like it was meant to be some sort of food truck, but the service window was shuttered and the lights were off.

Caine searched the square and only saw one solitary walker, head down, hurrying along the shop fronts without even looking at the display. A door opened briefly, and then the square was empty again.

Meaghan puffed out her cheeks. "And that's how you go from 'magical Christmas wonderland' to 'creepy haunted town' in one easy step, folks. Or from 'creepy haunted town' to 'festively lit and somehow even creepier haunted town'." She hesitated, her eyes glittering. "Ready for some more conspiracy theorizing?"

"Hit me." Caine's eyes were dazzled, but he hung on her every word.

"The Heartwell family always sponsors a Christmas tree for the town square. *One* tree. And now, the same year that visitors are down, tourist revenue is plummeting, and *no one* will admit that maybe there's something behind all the weird shit that's been driving people away… what do we get? Not one tree, but dozens, lighting up the square like someone's afraid of the dark."

A shiver went down Caine's spine. Meaghan raised one eyebrow.

"Too crazy?"

"Not at all. Except if that was the plan, it's not working, is it? No one's here."

"And the creepy factor grows." Meaghan scuffed her foot on the sidewalk. "Or maybe it's all just a terrible coincidence. Someone made a bad call and put more money into the town decorations fund the same year visitor numbers randomly go down, and all the weird shit that's been going on has nothing to do with it. There's no conspiracy to scare people away from Pine Valley."

"And if that's the case, then you've been going around kidnapping tourists for nothing."

Meaghan grimaced. "You have no idea what a freak I've been about this whole situation. I'm surprised—" She sighed. "Never mind. Come on. Let's go get your 'sorry I kidnapped you' dinner. Hannah's place should be open tonight and we don't need to worry about getting a table…"

Caine fell into step beside her as she headed across the square. He took a deep breath and the icy air stung his lungs.

What he'd told Meaghan was true: he was a city boy. He was used to snow and ice—but not being somewhere where the nearest centrally-heated building was farther away than the edge of the sidewalk. The icy air in his lungs was as biting as it could get in the city in winter, but it was a clean cold, with no lingering tang of pollution. Winter in Pine Valley was familiar and strange at the same time… and so was he.

Caine caught sight of himself in a dark window. Same reddish-brown hair and blue eyes, same pale skin and undefeatable shadow of stubble on his chin. But who was he really, now?

Not the same Caine he'd been last Christmas, before the hellhound had gotten its claws into him. Not the Caine he'd been for the last twelve months, fighting his way through a new, terrifying world.

Someone new.

The trees made it hard to see much of the buildings as they crossed the square. Caine glimpsed some wooden facades and smaller Christmas displays and decals on shop windows. And—

"What the hell is that?"

"I told you, it's the Heartwell—oh. That." Meaghan's voice fell. "It's—hey! Do you want to know, or not?"

She had to yell because Caine was already running. The patch of darkness he'd spotted through the trees pulled at him like a magnet. The deserted Christmas display might be eerie, but this shadow was *wrong*.

He skidded to a stop in front of what had looked from a distance like a brightly-colored streamer. The police tape was stretched across the front of a burned-out husk that must have once been a quaint shop like the others around the square.

Meaghan caught up to Caine and stood beside him, hands in her pockets and her breath puffing out in huge white clouds.

"That," she said, her voice hard, "is another *accident*."

Caine's nose wrinkled. The fire that had ripped through the building had happened long enough ago that there was a layer of snow on what was left of the walls, and inside, where it had fallen through the burnt-out holes in the roof. But the bitter smell of burning paint still lingered on the air.

"Was anyone hurt?"

"No, thank God. The shop had been closed for repairs. Then, the night before the big reopening—boom. Up in flames." Meaghan sighed. "All the new stock, all the work and money that went into fixing the place up... and only a week before Christmas."

"What sort of a store was it?" Caine knelt down. There was more than just a hint of fire and ash in the air; there was something else, something just out of reach of his human senses…

"Toys. Mr. Bell is—well, let's just say I wouldn't want to work for him, but he puts on a hell of a Santa Claus show for the kids. Like if the Grinch decided he liked Christmas after all but still was a total dick about it."

"A Christmas toy store."

Caine went very still. His breath steamed in the air.

"This happened a few days ago?"

"And today they hit the Puppy Express." Meaghan hissed with frustration. "If there *is* a they. If the men who stole the dogs today are the same people who've been behind everything else."

"They're escalating. Going from scaring people to endangering them."

Chasing them off. But why?

He rubbed the back of his neck at another prickle of familiarity. *It can't be… what you suspect. You're jumping to conclusions. Remember how badly that went back when you started out as a PI?*

Forget the supernatural side. Not everything in the world has to do with shifters.

Whoever's behind this, they're targeting the industry that keeps Pine Valley alive.

"You know what?" he said, standing up slowly and turning to face Meaghan.

Her eyes bored into his. There was a strange expression on her face: something vulnerable hiding behind the joking front she put on.

Caine was already determined to solve the mystery of Pine Valley, but that settled it. Meaghan was more than upset about what was happening here; it was hurting her. And he couldn't allow that.

"I think you're more right than you know. I think someone's

trying to ruin Christmas in Pine Valley."

Meaghan's lips parted. The vulnerable expression in her eyes turned hopeful.

"And I'm going to help you stop them."

CHAPTER SIX

Meaghan

I'm going to help you.

Caine's words fluttered around in Meaghan's mind like a feather caught in the wind, or dust motes in a beam of sunlight. She wanted to grab them and hold them tight—but she was scared that if she did, they'd disappear. Become less real.

Less wonderful.

"Here we are," she announced, leaving the words to flutter around free. "The Hearthstone Grill. If you haven't eaten since this morning, then—"

A loud rumble interrupted her. Caine made a face and rubbed his stomach. "It's true. I'd be starving in the snow without you."

Meaghan's cheeks heated up. Caine kept trying to spin the afternoon's events like she'd done him a favor instead of lost her freaking mind, and… it was nice. Dumb, but nice.

She pushed the door open.

"Come on, then."

It was so warm inside that Meaghan felt beads of moisture form on her upper lip. She licked them off and Caine made a strange noise. *Must be starving,* Meaghan thought, and was about to wave over one of the waitstaff when someone grabbed her around the waist.

"Evening, Mrs. Holborn," she gasped.

"Meaghan! Here for dinner? The usual? Sit up by the bar while I look after this gentleman here."

Hannah Holborn barely came up to Meaghan's elbow. She was in her sixties, with steel-gray hair, warm brown eyes and a tribe of grandchildren who all seemed to take it in turns to visit Pine Valley and let her bully them about their life choices.

She gave Meaghan one last grandmotherly squeeze and pushed her not-too-gently in the direction of the bar.

Meaghan's stomach clenched. Of course Hannah didn't think Caine was here with her. Meaghan had never brought any guys to the Grill—not that there'd been any guys for her to bring—and besides, Caine was... Caine. Striking. Gorgeous. Way out of her league.

"We're—" she began.

"Terence'll keep you company," Hannah said, giving her another shove. "Won't you, Terence?"

There was a young man already sitting at the bar. With his thick brown hair and spectacles, he had to be another one of the Holborn clan. He gave Meaghan a half-hearted wave.

Meaghan scrunched up her face. "Mrs. Holborn, I—"

"Now. Table for one, dear?" Hannah smoothed down her apron and smiled at Caine.

Caine smiled back. "Two, please. Though I'm happy to sit at the bar, if that's your usual?"

He directed the question at Meaghan. Hannah stared from him, to her, and connected the dots. Possibly more dots than actually existed.

"Oh! Oh-h-h-h." She grinned, and Meaghan's stomach

dropped.

She'd seen that look before, when Hannah was discussing her grandchildren's love lives.

Surely she couldn't think—he's way *out of my league! This isn't a date, it's a... an information-gathering meeting. For crazy conspiracy theorists. Who want to save Christmas from a pack of ghosts.*

"Actually the bar's closed," Hannah announced straight-faced. She flapped one hand behind her back. "Terence! Back in the kitchen. Now, a table for two..."

Her grin widened. Meaghan's stomach dropped even further. "Mrs. Holborn..."

"It's a beautiful night, isn't it? Why don't you both follow me upstairs."

"Mrs. Holborn, the bar's—"

"—Closed." Hannah's voice brooked no opposition. She gestured to the staircase at the back of the restaurant, and then to Caine to go ahead, and grabbed Meaghan's elbow to hiss in her ear: "You never introduced me to your *friend*, Meaghan!"

"I only met him today!"

"Hmph! Moving fast. Good. No point in wasting time with these things."

"I'm not—This isn't a—"

Meaghan's voice broke off as Hannah smacked her on the ass. She yelped and practically ran up the stairs.

The Grill's rooftop area was a maze of tiled courtyards that had been built into and around the terraced roof. Intimate tables were tucked in beside snow-covered eaves and roof tiles, heated by freestanding electric braziers.

Meaghan groaned as Hannah led them both to the prime spot overlooking the square. The romantic, lights-and-tree-filled square.

"Mrs. Holborn…"

"Shh, love. Leave it to me," Hannah whispered. Then, louder: "Drinks for you both to start?"

"Not for me." Meaghan rushed the words out and then blinked, surprised Hannah had let her finish the sentence. "Er, I'm driving. Caine's staying out in the valley."

Hannah's expression at *that* little tidbit would be seared into Meaghan's memory forever, filed under *Oh God why did I say that.*

"*Well.*" Hannah widened her eyes and, to Meaghan's horror, winked. "Why don't you both sit down and I'll see about some menus? Terence!"

She bustled away, leaving Meaghan feeling winded. She pressed her fingers against her eyes. "I am so sorry about that, Caine. Hannah—Mrs. Holborn—is…"

The scrape of chair legs made her open her eyes. Caine was standing behind the chair nearest to her. Holding it out for her.

"Mrs. Holborn seems like a very intelligent lady," he said. One corner of his mouth curled up and Meaghan's heart, already fluttering, started to thump.

Is that a real smile, or a fuck-you're-weird smile? Does it even matter?

She swallowed. There was no point in fooling herself. She'd found Caine… distracting… even when she thought he was a dog-stealing arsonist, and now? Her skin heated up every time he so much as glanced at her. He was funny, warm…

And he believes me about the ghost gang.

Which was all this was about, right? That curled half-smile, the way he was playing along with Hannah's mistaken idea that they were on some sort of a date—it had to be because finding out more about her crazy theory was more interesting than whatever business had brought him to Pine Valley.

Hell, traveling for business at Christmas? He must be longing for anything to distract him.

He's just some guy who was happily living his life before you bull-dozed your way into it. He's just...

Meaghan sat down and Caine gently pushed the chair in. She closed her eyes and groaned silently. *He's just the most amazing man you've ever met. And you ruined any chance you had with him before you even found out his name.*

She cracked one eye open. *Hang on...*

Caine sat down across the table and she cleared her throat. "I'm not sure we actually... Did I ever introduce myself?"

"No." Caine's eyes sparkled. "But I get the feeling it's 'Meaghan'? Or... 'Megs'?"

"Meaghan Markham. *Not* Megs. That's just Jackson trying to rile me up."

"Does it work?"

Meaghan snorted. "About as well as me hassling him about my conspiracy theories works to rile him up, so... yeah."

The restaurant door swung open and Hannah bustled over to the table, cradling a bottle under one arm.

Caine raised his eyebrows at Meaghan. "I thought you said you weren't drinking?"

"Ah, she's a big girl, she can have one drink with dinner and still drive." Hannah plonked the bottle on the table before Meaghan could object. "But you'll need something to help soak it up. Tonight's menu..."

"I'll have everything," Caine said quickly.

Hannah nodded. "Good, good. And you, Meaghan? The usual?"

"Thanks, Mrs. Holborn."

Hannah gave Meaghan a wink that made her cheeks burn and

went back inside. Meaghan glared at the bottle of—holy crap, was that *actual* champagne?—and tried to pull her scrambled thoughts together.

"Your gran's not exactly subtle, is she?"

Meaghan blinked. "What? Mrs. Holborn isn't my grandmother."

"Ah. Sorry. I remember now." Caine's smile made Meaghan want to sigh and melt onto the floor. "One of your bad ideas: moving to a town where you don't know anyone."

"Come New Year's, I'll have been here just about six months."

"I never would have guessed. Everyone I've seen here acts as if they've known you forever."

"Well, when you've got as much practice pushing yourself in where you're not wanted as I do, these things come naturally." Meaghan caught Caine's questioning expression and sucked in her lower lip.

Might as well come out and say it.

She tapped her palms on the table. "Foster kid for life, that's me. Trust me, when you're a tiny fish in a big pond, you'll do anything to stand out. Up to supergluing yourself to someone and telling them it means you're friends now."

Caine chuckled. "I can't imagine you as a tiny fish."

"Oh, I was. Then puberty hit. Suddenly I didn't need to jump for people to see me." She paused. "Didn't stop me jumping, though." *Even though things that seemed cute when you were a knobbly-kneed tyke make you a pain in the ass now you're all grown up.*

"That must have been hard." Caine's eyes were soft, staring into hers, and *that* was new. Usually people got so awkward they wouldn't even look at her. Which never actually stopped her telling the story.

That's me. Foster kid always pushing myself in where I'm not wanted and making other people uncomfortable... Yeah, I might know where my issues come from, but that doesn't mean I'm over them.

"Well, better to have five or ten temporary families than none at all, right?" she said lightly.

"Perhaps."

Something in Caine's voice made her freeze. *Oh shit. What have I said now? Families—better than having none at all... Oh, God, girl, how could you be so stupid?*

Her horror must have shown on her face. Caine held up a hand as she sputtered out an apology.

"I'm sorry—I didn't think—"

"I was thinking there's another option. A family that might as well not exist. My parents are both still alive, but they might as well be on the Moon for all I see them." His mouth twisted. "And maybe that's a good thing."

"What do you mean?"

A family who was *hers*, but stayed far enough away that she couldn't ruin things with them? Caine had just described the most Meaghan-proof option in the world.

"My parents might not have been worth writing home about, but I had a good friend who was as close as a brother to me. And... things didn't exactly work out."

It might have been the flickering lights from the braziers, but Caine looked pale. Meaghan wanted to reach out and comfort him. She sat on her hands as he rubbed his face and groaned.

"Sorry. That got heavy fast, didn't it? What was I—oh, I remember." Caine rested his cheek on one hand and gave her a rueful smile. "I was about to give you a comforting speech about how I never would have guessed you'd only been in Pine Valley six months, and the best family is the one you build yourself, and if Mrs. Holborn isn't your gran, then—"

He broke off and made a strange noise. Meaghan blinked. It sounded like a *growl*. A whiny growl, the sort Parkour or Lolly would make when they thought they weren't getting their fair share of pets.

"Excuse me?" she said.

"Er." Caine cleared his throat. "Can I pour you a drink?"

"Go ahead."

Meaghan watched Caine fill her glass. The champagne fizzed, catching the firelight.

He frowned at his own glass as he filled it. Meaghan leaned forward.

"Then...?"

"Hmm?"

"I mean, great speech so far, but you need to work on your closing remarks. 'Then' leaves a lot of room for confusion."

Caine looked strangely displeased. For a moment she thought he was going to change the subject, then he sighed. "*Then*, if Mrs. Holborn isn't your gran... she must have been trying to set you up with her grandson back there in the bar. Terence."

Meaghan burst out laughing. "She *what*? Oh my God, Caine, that's ridiculous. Besides, I've met... all of her grandsons..."

"How many does she have?"

"Nine." Meaghan grimaced as a few memories rose to the surface. "I've had awkward drinks with the whole set, except for Terence, and I think I've just realized *why* they were so awkward."

Caine swore. When Meaghan raised her eyebrows at him, he grimaced.

"What?"

"First I let my family problems take over the speech, and now my jealousy's coming along for the ride." Caine shut his eyes and leaned back in his chair. Then he cracked one eye open. "Can I try again? I think I can do a better job of the speech this time."

"Which one?" Meaghan's heart felt like it was about to leap out of her chest. She wasn't sure whether it was nerves, or excitement.

Caine leaned forward. His chair legs clacked on the floor. He put his elbows on the table and locked eyes with Meaghan.

"Meaghan, I—"

The restaurant door banged. "Dinner!" Hannah caroled, sidling between the long tables with a plate balanced on each hand. Terence trundled along behind her, his arms stacked with plates.

"You did say 'everything', doll." Hannah winked at Caine as she deposited the first two plates and then started unloading Terence. "And business is down so we have a lot of extra this week that needs eating up. I hope you're hungry!"

"Starved." Caine was still staring straight at Meaghan, but his gaze wavered as the table filled with food. "Is this all for us?"

"You did order everything," Meaghan reminded him.

When Hannah and Terence were gone, Meaghan's mind lurched back to what Caine had been saying. She licked her lips.

Jealousy? But… first, there's no way Hannah's been trying to set me up with any of her grandsons. She's just… generally grandmotherly. And even if she had been… if Caine was jealous of that… then that means…

Meaghan's mouth was dry. She cleared her throat.

"So," Caine said, his eyes glittering in the firelight. "About that speech…"

"You really feel jeal—you really think people here like me?" Meaghan winced.

She'd almost said it. Why hadn't she? She always jumped in. Pushed in. Threw herself at whatever bad decision came into her head. So why was she shying away from talking to Caine about his "jealousy"?

"I do."

Meaghan met his gaze. His eyes were clear and warm.

"Well you're wrong." Meaghan rubbed her eyes and looked away. "Maybe they liked me for a while. These last few months have fixed that."

"Your investigations into all the 'accidents'?" Caine's eyebrows drew together. He balanced his chin on one fist, leaning forward, all his attention on Meaghan. She squirmed under it.

"Yeah."

Meaghan waited for a wave of relief at avoiding the whole "jealousy" subject, but it didn't come. She stared at the bubbles popping in her glass of champagne.

"When I first moved here, everyone was so welcoming. But as soon as I started talking about how I thought there was something weird going on, they all clammed up. And the more they clam up the more I feel like there has to be something wrong, something they're not telling me, and I—"

She clenched her fists and then let them go, her shoulders sagging.

"It's *bad*. The Puppy Express usually has way more seasonal staff, from what Bob's said, but it's just Olly and me this year. Hannah's had to lay people off. And that's just two businesses. It's the same all over town. I'm worried that if no one does anything, then it won't just be Christmas that's ruined."

"It'll be all of Pine Valley."

Meaghan's lips parted. She stared at Caine. "That's right!"

He sees what I see. And he's not looking at me like I'm crazy. He's looking at me like he's—

Her phone chimed. She pulled it out of her pocket, her cheeks burning. "It's Jackson."

"Aren't you going to answer?"

Meaghan snorted. "Jackson knows better than to call me, after the first ten times I talked his ear off about my ghost gang conspiracy. He's sent a text."

She held her phone across the table Caine read out:

"Sleigh safe. Forest safe. Olly says how is dinner." He raised his eyebrows. "Man of few words, isn't he?"

"Wait, Olly's with him?" Meaghan snatched her phone back. "Does that mean—because they'd be *perfect* together, and… no. I am not going to text him about it. Or her. Or…" Her eyes widened. "He said 'Forest safe'. He wouldn't say that unless there was a possibility it *wasn't* safe. If he thought there was nothing to worry about, he would have made it into a joke, or not said anything."

"He thinks whoever took the dogs is dangerous."

"If I can convince him that it's not just today, that everything that happened *before* now is connected—" Meaghan's fingers were already flying over the screen.

Caine put his hand over hers. His fingers were warm.

"You really want to risk interrupting their date?"

The slight emphasis on the word 'their' made Meaghan pause.

Their date.

Or… *our* date?

She gulped.

"Maybe I should… hold off. For now?" she stuttered. "Um. We should eat, and come up with a plan, and… talk."

Caine's eyes gleamed. He lifted his glass and clinked it against hers.

"To talking."

"And not running in and messing things up before they're even

58

had a chance to start."

Like... whatever this is, she thought. *This not even a maybe... date.*

CHAPTER SEVEN

Caine

Caine's mind was whirring. Without his demon constantly taking up half of his attention, he felt more clear-headed than ever. Like a new man.

Unfortunately, one of the things his clear-headedness was making obvious was that Meaghan's tendency to throw herself at things didn't include him. At least, not now that she no longer suspected him of being a dog-napper.

She seemed interested. He thought. Or maybe it was just that he hoped she did.

A year out of the dating scene and I'm rusty as hell, he thought glumly.

"Mmf."

Caine groaned and closed his eyes. Time was running out for him to figure out whether Meaghan felt the same way about him as he did about her. They were halfway back to his ski cottage, and every time the truck lumbered over a pothole or around a tricky corner, Meaghan made that tiny squeak-grunt that went straight down his spine to… places that weren't particularly well-disguised by his flimsy sweatpants.

He cleared his throat and adjusted his position as much as he could, crammed into the passenger seat. The headlights illuminated something ahead.

"Watch out—pothole."

"Got it." Meaghan yanked on the steering wheel. "*Mmf.* What were you saying?"

"Does the Puppy Express have CCTV?"

"What, like security cameras? Why—" Meaghan gasped and hauled on the steering wheel again. "Of course! If there's footage of the assholes who stole the dogs. Which... I probably should have checked out, before I went haring off into the woods. Or at least asked Olly for some descriptions."

"I'm glad you didn't."

"So you keep insisting..." Meaghan glanced at him, her honey-colored eyes half-suspicious, half-amused.

Amused. Caine's heart leapt. That was better than a glare, wasn't it?

"Why are you so interested, anyway? You with the FBI or something?" She'd said it jokingly, but then her eyes widened. "Oh my God... you're not, are you?"

Caine laughed. "Oh no. Nothing so grand. But I did used to work as a private investigator. And before you start thinking smoky nightclubs and trench coats, I was more the spend-three-weeks-poring-over-building-permits-in-the-city-records sort of investigator."

"No battles of wits with sexy femmes fatales?"

"Not until tonight."

Meaghan's mouth dropped open. She shut it quickly, but her eyes were shining in a way that gave Caine hope.

"Well, um. Huh. So, is that what brought you here? You're going to spend Christmas squinting at old records? Wait. You said 'building permits'. You're not with all those property investors who've been sniffing around, are you?"

"I'm not here with anyone." *Property investors. Huh. Another piece of the puzzle?*

"They were all over the place when I first moved here. I ended up sleeping on Olly's sofa for a while because there were literally no spare rooms in town. Uh, and because I showed up at her house with all my stuff."

"Did they get any bites? I'm guessing not."

Meaghan shot him a strange look. "No, they didn't. How did you know?"

Because I've seen how this sort of shit goes down. Caine rubbed his head.

"Like I said. I've read a *lot* of very boring property archives. Small towns tend to circle the wagons when people come in flashing their cash around, wanting to buy up land."

Especially if your town's home to a family of dragons.

He crooked an eyebrow at Meaghan as a thought struck him. "You didn't have any problems like that?"

"No, I was saved by the fact I don't have any wads of cash to throw around. Lucky me. And poor Olly, getting paid sofa-rent in my cooking." She sighed. "I'm in the running for coal in my stocking this year, with what a bad friend I've been. I'm glad Jackson's with her tonight at least. I feel like such a jerk for leaving her this morning."

"What happened this morning, anyway? You never said." Caine leaned forward. "It might help us piece together what's going on."

Meaghan pinched her lips thin. "I got to work late. Truck threw a hissy fit—literally. I was already in a bad mood by the time I got in but then I saw Olly and..." She grimaced. "She's always so in control. A bit weird—she has this *thing* about seeing people first before they see her, I swear, one time we went for drinks in town and she scoped out the bar through literally every window before she would go in…" Meaghan sighed and shook her head. "Sorry, I'm getting off-topic."

"Don't mind—log!—it's a long drive." Caine braced himself as Meaghan swerved to avoid the log.

"And you need something to keep your mind off your cramped knees? All right." Meaghan hunched into her shoulders as she encouraged the truck up the slope. "Come on, come on… mmf! Yes!"

Caine closed his eyes briefly. That noise technically was helping keep his mind off his knees, but in other very real ways it was not helping at all.

"She was shaking like a leaf. Said she caught some guys creeping around. They hadn't touched her, but she said there was something about the way they looked that just… freaked her out. I don't know if they were in masks, or…"

"Wait. The way they looked, or the way they looked at her?"

Caine's blood ran cold. Maybe he'd been too hasty to assume that the criminals weren't supernatural.

Because if there was one thing that cemented his hellhound's evil in his mind beyond all doubt, it was the fact that it terrified people. The rest of him could be human-shaped, but if his hellhound looked out through his eyes, it was like it bored through their minds straight to the things that scared them the most.

"She said she felt like her skull had been scraped out with a rusty knife covered in acid. But—but she also said she was fine, and I shouldn't worry about it, and Bob was due back from checking the routes in a few minutes, so…"

"You ran straight after them." *The men who'd scared your friend and stolen your dogs. And who might not be men at all.*

Caine didn't know if he was more impressed, or terrified. If his suspicions were correct, and the thieves were anything like what he suspected...

It's a damned good thing she found me first.

He shook his head. Meaghan was hellhound Kryptonite, he'd proved that.

"I should have been at work earlier. I should—I'll call her tomorrow. Make sure she's okay, then take her out for drinks and force her to tell me *everything* about tonight." She wrinkled her nose happily. "At least that's one good thing to come out of all of this."

"Not the only good thing." Caine gazed at her until she glanced at him. She looked away quickly, her eyebrows drawing together... and a smile curving her lips.

Yes! Caine thought silently. *Not so rusty after all.*

"Oh? You can think of some other things, huh?" Meaghan didn't even look at him, but from the way she put her chin up, it was a very deliberate not-looking.

"One or two. Such as that dinner... oh God." He sat bolt upright. "Wait a minute. Did you pay for dinner?"

Meaghan snickered. "I didn't see you pulling your wallet out. And I'm not sure where you would have pulled it out from, either, with what you were wearing earlier." She bit her tongue before another chuckle escaped. "Don't worry, Hannah let me put it on my tab. And she didn't charge me for that bottle of wine, either."

"Thank you. I'll go into town tomorrow and sort it out."

"You'll what?"

"I'll pay off—"

"No. Oh, no, Mr. Private Investigator. You listening to me rave on about invisible thieves trying to ruin Christmas is worth more

64

than one dinner."

Her lips pinched together just for a second, and Caine wondered with a lurch just how much of a dent his "ordering everything" had made in her wallet.

"Does that mean you'll take me out again tomorrow?" he teased. *And I'll sort out that tab with Mrs. Holborn.*

Meaghan narrowed her eyes and sucked in her lips, but nothing could disguise the delighted grin sneaking across her face.

"You know, I'm driving here."

"Uh-huh."

"Concentrating on the road."

"I see."

"It's important that you don't distract me."

"Of course."

He waited another minute as the truck bumped up the road.

"So that's a yes?"

Meaghan clicked her tongue and nodded out the window. "Maybe. Let's see if I still have a job tomorrow, first. By the way, you recognize anything out there yet?"

Caine looked around. "Er... we're on a road?" They'd been at the restaurant for hours; night had well and truly fallen and the moon was barely breaking through the trees. "A road with trees."

Then the trees thinned. The moon poured its light over the snowy ground, turning it silver. A small building sat in the middle of the clearing. It wasn't as quaintly old-fashioned as most of the other buildings around Pine Valley; it was wooden, but the design was modern, with sharp angles and lots of triple-glazed glass.

Home, Caine's heart whispered. He frowned. He'd barely spent an hour at the ski cottage awake; he didn't know where the light switches were, or the cutlery, or how the washer worked. It wasn't *home*. Home was...

A bare apartment in a big, faceless city, a year ago. He'd been too busy with work to furnish it and make it feel lived in. Or even to live in it much. He'd spent so many late evenings at the office, too many of which had turned into nights spent curled up under his desk.

This rented cottage was the first place he'd heard Meaghan's voice. The place he'd been living when he was finally freed from his demon.

Caine breathed deep. Maybe this was home. Or the closest thing he had to it. For now.

Maybe now that he was a normal guy again, he could be one of those assholes who flashed wads of cash around and try to buy the cottage. Make it his real home.

"I don't think my truck's going to take that driveway. Do you want a hand bringing in the leftovers?"

Caine opened his mouth to say he could manage… then thought better. "Thanks," he said instead. A few more minutes with Meaghan… he'd be an idiot to turn down that opportunity.

The truck's engine croaked as Meaghan turned it off. Caine darted out to open the driver's side door for her, and made sure she only had one bag to carry up to the cottage.

Her eyebrows shot up. "I can handle carrying more than a single loaf of bread, Caine. Come on."

Hannah had been more than generous with the leftovers. The "everything" Caine had ordered had been more than too much for them both to get through on its own, but he suspected that the bags and bags of meat, vegetables, bread, eggs, coffee and milk—not to mention the remaining half-bottle of champagne— was more than had been on the table at the restaurant.

"I need you to have a hand free," he explained, and reached into his pocket. He frowned. "Hang on."

Meaghan watched him with an amused expression on her face. "Missing something?"

"My keys." Caine swore. "I should have seen this coming. No wallet. No key. No phone, to call the rental agency…" He stared up at the cottage.

"Doesn't look like you left the door open," Meaghan said. She grabbed another bag out of his arms and walked up the drive. "But it might not be locked, still."

Caine trailed behind her. "I, uh, didn't take the door."

"What?"

A few minutes later, Caine was grappling with the balcony railing. Meaghan's laughter drifted up from below him.

"I can't believe you jumped off the balcony," Meaghan called out between laughs. "How did you not break both your legs?"

"Can we save the questions for when I'm not dangling for my life?" Caine jack-knifed one leg over the railing and pulled himself over. He landed on the balcony with a huff. "Down in a minute!"

His heart was pounding, and not just from his climb up the side of the cottage. The balcony door was wide open. He pulled it shut, and then watched with a muttered curse as it popped itself open again. He tried again, turning the lock this time, and again, it gently clicked open.

Caine half-laughed, half-groaned. *So that's what started all of this. A broken door.*

He wedged it shut and headed for the stairs. Halfway across the room, his eyes caught on the bed. The blankets were still tangled, and he couldn't help thinking about how Meaghan would look tangled up in them.

Meaghan. God, Meaghan. Everything about her made him want to know more about her.

Outside, she was still wearing her bulky winter coat—fully

buttoned, unlike his, which he'd again forgotten to do up—and the hat that hid all but one stray curl of her hair. She'd taken her gloves off to drive, but they were back on now. She was completely covered up and she was still the sexiest woman he'd ever seen.

But Meaghan was more than that. She was a raging inferno of energy, of incredible passion. It roared up in her eyes whenever she talked about the dog-thieves and the havoc they'd caused in Pine Valley.

I guess I like a woman who takes charge. He chuckled to himself. *And isn't afraid to shove a man into the trunk of her car to get things done.*

Meaghan was fiery, and obstinate, and left people stunned in her wake. Caine included. But he didn't want to be left in her wake. He wanted to be beside her, hunting out the wrongdoers who had harmed her people.

Caine paused before he unlocked the front door. There was another reason he wanted to spend more time with Meaghan. He almost hated himself for admitting it.

The demon hound inside him had only fled at Meaghan's touch. What if it came back when she left?

His hand clenched on the door handle. *That's not going to happen. It didn't come back when I climbed up onto the balcony, did it? And it's not like we've been joined at the hip since she grabbed me the first time. Whatever this town did, or she did… it's done.*

I'm free.

He opened the door.

CHAPTER EIGHT

Meaghan

Oh, God, he's so hot.

Meaghan squeezed her eyes shut. *What's wrong with you? He's been out of your sight for, what, five minutes?*

You have it bad, girl.

"Everything all right?"

Meaghan's eyes snapped open. "Fine! Fine. Why would there be a problem?"

Apart from the fact that you're the most gorgeous guy I ever met and... and we still haven't talked about that whole "jealous" thing. Her heart thudded. *And he asked me to dinner. Again. He knows what a crazy weirdo I am, and he wants to see more of me.*

Okay. Yep. Running safely away from that one, not straight into it like your usual bull-headed self.

"With your eyes all screwed up I thought you might have a headache. Here, I'll take the bags."

Meaghan handed them to him. *The only headache here is me.*

Caine looked back over his shoulder. "Do you want to come in?"

"I..."

Yes! Meaghan's body and a great deal of her mind was screaming. *Yes! Go in!*

If this was any other situation, any other night and any other person, she would have done it without thinking. But Caine...

"I should go," she finished, staring at her toes. "I—it's late, and I, um... have work... you know, unless Bob decides to fire me for today."

"I doubt he'll do that."

Caine's eyes were sincere. But that only meant he thought he was telling the truth. Meaghan knew better: sooner or later she pushed too hard, and people got sick of her and then it was off to the next home for her. She'd been nearing that with Pine Valley for weeks now, and this afternoon would surely have pushed things over the edge.

"Well. If I don't turn up early tomorrow then he definitely will," she said, forcing a smile. Caine grimaced in agreement. "Don't get me wrong. Tonight was..."

The expression in Caine's eyes sent warmth flooding through her veins. She looked away, biting her lip.

"It's nice not being the only crazy person in Pine Valley who believes in the ghost gang. Though I do still think that you acting like me kidnapping you was a good thing is going to do terrible things to my personality. Like I told you, I'm bad enough without that sort of encouragement." Meaghan took a deep breath and firmed up her shoulders. "So... sleep well. I promise not to wake you up by yelling outside of your window this time."

"Shame." Caine grinned. Meaghan glared at him, and he only grinned wider. "You never gave me a straight answer outside. When will I see you again?"

Meaghan's glare froze.

"If I can't rely on you kidnapping me, I feel like we need to make a plan. Or I need to get your phone number at least."

"I…" she began, and froze.

Say no. Say no and keep this one perfect night intact. If you keep going, then when everything goes wrong, you won't be able to look back on tonight without remembering how you ruined it after.

Except… he's asking for business reasons, right? That must be it. He's helping me investigate the ghost gang. That's all. So really, you refusing *to get his number would be the weird thing to do.*

Meaghan's head was spinning. She wanted so much for Caine's interest in her to be more than just her connection to Pine Valley's freaky ghost mystery.

She pulled out her phone.

"Here you go," she said in what she hoped was a casual manner, handing him her phone. *Just for business. Nothing more. And if I do call him, and he doesn't pick up, I can always go hide in a cave somewhere until he leaves Pine Valley.*

"Message me in the morning?" Caine's eyes sparkled.

"Sure," Meaghan squeaked. "If you want to meet Olly properly and talk to her about what she saw, I can organize…"

"I was thinking more for breakfast. The two of us."

That doesn't sound like just business.

Meaghan licked her lips. She felt like she was standing on the edge of a cliff. If she blurted out something stupid now, sure, she'd know either way whether Caine was meaning a business breakfast or something… more. Except after her blurting, he probably wouldn't want either.

Or…

Maybe she didn't have to ruin this. Maybe, for once in her life, she could control her hell-sent tendencies to rush at life like a bull in a china shop. She could come up with a plan, couldn't she? Some strategies for acting like a normal person? The sort of person Caine might want to spend more time with? For business, or… other reasons?

"Okay," she said, and this was already a bad idea because forget controlling her bullheadedness, she couldn't even control her face enough to keep a stupid smile from spreading across it. "Tomorrow."

"Great." Caine's smile was addictive. She felt a giggle bubbling up her throat.

It was definitely time to leave.

"Okay. I'll just… bye." Meaghan pushed her hands deep into her pockets and spun around. She trudged down the end of the drive to her truck, ears straining.

She didn't hear the cottage door shut until she was at her truck.

"Argh," she moaned once she was sure Caine wasn't watching her anymore. "*A-a-a-argh.*"

She jabbed the key at the ignition, managing to get it in on the third try. "Argh!"

The truck groaned as she turned the key. The engine whined— and whined—and fell silent.

This seriously can't be happening.

Meaghan threw her head back. So much for going home and strategizing.

"Shit."

CHAPTER NINE

Caine

Caine closed the door and leaned against it, eyes closed. He couldn't get Meaghan's face out of his head: the way she'd ducked her head, the smile she hadn't been able to hide. The sheer, surprised delight shining out of her eyes.

Tomorrow.

For the first time in a year, he was looking to the future with excitement, not fear.

I'll see her tomorrow. And the next day and, please God, the day after that.

He let his head rest back against the door, running over the evening's conversation in his head. Remembering every expression that had flitted across Meaghan's face. Every spark of passion and determination behind her eyes.

And, of course, what they'd been talking about. One name stood out in particular. *Heartwell.* If his demon was going to raise its head at anything, it would have been Meaghan mentioning that name. It hadn't even pricked an ear. It was gone.

Jasper Heartwell was the man he'd come here to see. The shifter, he should say. The dragon shifter who'd almost lost his dragon.

Caine sketched out a plan in his head as he put the bags of food in the kitchen. He'd call Heartwell tomorrow. Tell him to put a rain check on their meeting. When he first contacted Jasper Heartwell, Caine had been wary to reveal too much of exactly what he needed help with, in case his hellhound was listening—now he was glad he'd obscured the truth. His nightmare was over and the fewer people who knew about it the better.

And after he'd called Heartwell, he'd see Meaghan again.

Warmth spread through his limbs. He'd see Meaghan again and they'd spend another evening like this one. Another evening where he didn't have to scrape himself to the bone with watchfulness. Another evening where he got to see Meaghan close her eyes with enjoyment as she devoured a slice of pie.

Except this time, he'd remember to bring his goddamn wallet.

He patted his pockets. *Where the hell is it?* He must have dumped it and his phone before he passed out that morning. Keys, too. All the paraphernalia of normal life.

Hmm.

When Meaghan had mentioned calling Olly in the morning to check on her, a thought had stirred in Caine's mind.

Angus Parker.

Angus was the friend he'd told Meaghan about, the one who was closer to him than his actual family. Or he had been, until the first thing Caine's hellhound did was attack him.

Caine didn't remember what happened after he transformed that time. The only memory he had was Angus' face twisting with fear. And since then, even thinking about Angus had set the hellhound off. Caine had had to push his old friend out of his mind. He'd never even gotten in contact with him to find out how he was doing.

The only reason Caine knew his old friend was still alive was that he'd locked himself in an abandoned basement one night and looked him up online. The battle to keep his hellhound under control had taken him weeks to recover from, but at least he'd gotten confirmation that Angus was still alive.

But, hell. A grin spread across Caine's face. It was Christmas. His hellhound was gone.

He could call Angus.

Assuming he could find his phone.

Caine padded up the stairs. It had to be in the bedroom, surely—unless he'd left it in the car? No—there it was, the screen cracked from when he'd kicked over the side table. He checked that it was still working.

I'll have to make sure I keep it charged, he told himself. *For when Meaghan messages me.*

He brought up his contacts list and his thumb hovered over Angus' name.

I know he's alive. But I don't know what my hellhound did after it attacked him. What if he's spent the last year trapped by his own monster, the same as me?

Guilt twisted in Caine's gut. *That's even more reason to contact him. My hellhound isn't a danger to him anymore, and no one should have to go through what I did alone.*

He tapped on Angus' name.

The phone rang. And rang. Then—

The call connected with a burst of static and a noise like Angus was still fumbling with his phone.

"Hey, sorry for keeping you hanging! I didn't have my phone on me—"

"Angus," Caine burst out. "Christ. It's me. I know it's been ages, I—"

"—and I still don't! Haha! Sorry, whoever you are, I'm gonna have to call you back. You know the drill. Leave a message after the…"

BEEP.

Caine let out a heavy breath and sat down on the end of the bed. Talking was one thing. Leaving a message was another.

"Hey, Angus," he said, just before the silence stretched out too long for him to bear. "It's me. Caine. I know it's been a long time and we didn't exactly part on…" He buried his head in his hands and groaned.

He'd stayed away from other shifters ever since he'd gotten his hellhound and learned shifters existed. All his focus had been on finding a way to get rid of the hellhound. But while he might not have learned much about other shifters, he knew they did everything they could to keep their existence secret from humans.

"Christ. I don't even know if you want to hear from me, but here it is. Things changed for me, last year, and now they've changed back. If you know what I'm talking about then you know what that means, and… and there's hope for you, too."

And if my hellhound didn't turn you into one, too, and you've written off my hellhound attacking you as a bad trip, then you'll probably think I've lost my goddamned mind when you listen to this.

He cleared his throat. "Either way, I'm back. Or close enough. I'm out of town at the moment, but I'm ready to get back into things. Might even pick up that property scam case I was working, back before… Anyway. Good talking at you, Angus. Merry Christmas."

He set the phone down and stared out through the window at the snow-covered mountains.

Everything was going to work out. He was going to be himself again, be *human* again, and then—maybe, now that there was more to him than endless watchful fear, now he had something to offer other than nightmares and exhaustion, maybe, Meaghan would—

Three knocks reverberated through the house.

Caine stood up. *Someone's at the door? But—*

He went back down the stairs. Too slowly, apparently, because after a very brief pause there were another three knocks. And another.

He opened the door and found Meaghan on the other side, one hand up to knock again.

Her chin was up, and the corners of her mouth were drawn tightly in.

"I swear I'm not doing this on purpose," she said, her eyes daring him to call her bluff.

Caine raised one eyebrow and was rewarded with a glare. The tension at the corners of her lips melted away.

"Not doing what on purpose? Knocking on my door?"

"I—guh. My truck won't start," Meaghan admitted through gritted teeth.

"So you're stuck and want me to help out with your truck. Hmm. Where have I heard that before?"

"That's why I said I wasn't doing this on purpose!" Meaghan groaned and pressed the heels of her hands against her temples. "There wouldn't be any point shoving you in the truck again anyway. The engine's had it. Won't even turn over."

Excitement shivered up Caine's spine. He crossed his arms, trying to act casual. "If you wanted to stay a bit longer, you just needed to say, you know."

"I..." Meaghan looked panicked, and Caine uncrossed his arms.

Act casual? What the hell was he thinking?

Meaghan took a deep breath and squeezed her eyes closed. "I

don't—*guh*—I don't want to be a nuisance and I don't want you to think…"

"Meaghan." Caine reached for her hand. Her fingers tightened around his and he licked his suddenly dry lips. "In the minute between us saying goodbye and you appearing here on my doorstep again, did you convince yourself I'd been lying about wanting to see you again?"

Meaghan's mouth dropped open. She shut it with a snap. "Yes," she admitted, and then rallied: "I told you, it's all-or-nothing with me."

"And I'm nothing?"

The words were out before he could stop them. Luckily, Meaghan seemed to be having the same problem.

"No!" She slapped her hand over her mouth and groaned. "You're not nothing. But I… I don't want to screw this up. I wanted time to, to…"

Caine leaned closer to her. That indignant "No!" made his heart leap. "I wish you'd throw yourself at me with as much reckless abandon as you do everything else in your life."

His breath froze in his throat. Meaghan's eyes widened until they filled his entire world, a thousand emotions tangling together behind them. Shock. Surprise. A single moment of delight, and then…

"What if I screw it up?"

"You won't."

She snorted half-heartedly. "You don't know me. I *always* screw it up."

Caine's skin prickled with cold. He stepped closer to Meaghan, until his breath made the fur lining of her hood shiver.

"I don't believe you."

Meaghan scraped her toe on the step. "I guess it's not like I have any other choice, with my truck broken down."

Caine glanced sideways. The rental car he'd driven here was just visible in the carport along the side of the cottage. Meaghan followed his gaze.

"Huh."

"It's up to you," Caine said quietly.

Meaghan bit her bottom lip. Her eyes searched Caine's, and then unfocused, as though she was thinking so hard she wasn't seeing anything.

At last she took a deep breath. "Okay. Let's recap. My truck's broken down. I'm a terrible mechanic. I only know enough to know it's stuffed."

"I hardly know one end of an engine from the other," Caine added helpfully. "And I expect the service station's closed, this late at night."

Meaghan bit down harder on her lower lip, but it didn't hide the smile pulling at the edges of her mouth. A thrill went through him.

"Definitely closed. And it would take him an hour to drive out here, which would make it tomorrow anyway." Meaghan took a deep breath and shuffled sideways, effectively blocking Caine's rental car from his sight. "I literally can't see any other way I can get back to town tonight."

Caine made a show of looking around the clearing in front of the cottage. His heart was singing. "I can't see anything, either."

"Well then." Meaghan narrowed her eyes at him. "I guess my only option is *all*, after all. Are you going to invite me in, or leave me out here to freeze?"

*

"It's *freezing* in here!" Meaghan wrapped her arms around herself and stamped her socked feet on the carpet. "Is the central heating broken? Maybe we should call someone after all."

Caine winced. He'd left the balcony door open that morning—and again just now when he'd climbed into the house—and now the entire cottage was frigid.

"My fault," he admitted. "I'll fix that right now."

He raced upstairs and closed the door, then paused to check the thermostat. When he got back to the living room, Meaghan was standing in front of the window. With the lights on inside, the trees were a ghostly shadow behind the room's reflection, and her reflected face was overlaid with snowy tree branches.

"It's gorgeous out here. I haven't been out this way much. Although..."

Meaghan hesitated, then put her hands to the glass and peered through them.

"Those trees look embarrassingly familiar."

Forgetting his quest, Caine stood beside her and pretended to squint out the window. Pretended, because that would have required tearing his eyes away from Meaghan.

"If you look closely you might see where I ran through them this morning. A man-shaped hole in the snow."

Meaghan half-snorted, half-groaned. "Bare footprints, because you didn't even stop to put your boots on..."

I wouldn't have stopped for anything. "And a good thing, too. If I'd wasted time with socks and shoes, you might have already been flattened by the sleigh by the time I got there. I wouldn't have even seen you."

"You have an answer for everything, don't you? To hear you say it, today wasn't just one screw-up after another. Everything happened for a reason."

"Didn't it?" Caine crossed the living room and stood beside her. His reflection brushed up against hers in the window. "I think everything's turned out incredibly well."

"Oh really? Even your light-up boots?"

"What's wrong with my boots?" Caine stamped his heels so the lights along the sides twinkled and Meaghan groaned.

"You know, there's a reason Bob let you take them for free. I don't think we ever sold a pair in men's sizes. Except to Jasper Heartwell last year."

Heartwell again. Caine shrugged the name aside.

Meaghan looked up from Caine's twinkling boots and gasped. The dramatically pained expression on her face was replaced by genuine tension. "Oh God."

"What is it?" Caine turned around, automatically putting himself between Meaghan and whatever she'd seen. He hadn't noticed anything as he came in, but he'd run upstairs and come back down with his mind full of Meaghan. The house could have been on fire and he wouldn't have noticed.

What he saw made him swallow back a curse. The nearest sofa had been pushed over. Its cushions were scattered around the room, and over the coffee table, which had been shoved awkwardly to one side. A throw rug had been dragged across the floor towards the stairs that led up to the bedroom. Caine vaguely recalled kicking something out of the way as he'd raced up them earlier.

And...

Oh.

Meaghan pushed past him. "Jackson was wrong. Someone has been here. The ghost gang—shit. I'd better call him."

"Don't." Something in Caine's heart rebelled at the thought of inviting Jackson into his home—no, the cottage—when Meaghan had only just got here. Besides... "This wasn't the ghost gang."

Meaghan spun around, eyes wide. "How do you know?" she demanded.

"Because I—argh. You remember I told you I drove all night to get here. I was pretty out of it by the time I arrived, and..."

"*You* made all this *mess?*" Meaghan's eyebrows shot together.

Caine gulped. "Well, I, er..."

Caine vaguely remembered dragging his luggage into the house, and then warding off another of the monster's attacks before he collapsed in bed.

He didn't realize he'd left the place such a dump. It hadn't seemed important at the time.

Because the idea that I'd be bringing a gorgeous woman home to a house that's in worse shape than my college dorm was the farthest thing from my mind.

"Is this your suitcase?" Meaghan was behind one of the sofas now.

"Er—"

"And your boots! You're still wearing them! Why didn't you take them off in the mudroom? You've tracked dirt all in!"

"Only from the car!" Caine yelped defensively.

Meaghan rose up from behind the sofa, her eyes mischievous. "You really are a city boy."

Caine ran one hand over his mouth and jaw, gathering up what dignity he had left after that indignant yelp. He had to fix this, goddammit.

"Right," he said, drawing himself up. Meaghan was still kneeling behind the sofa; she rested her elbows on it and grinned at him. "Here's what we're going to do. There must be one room in this house I haven't gone through like a tornado. If you would, please..."

He walked across the room, Meaghan's soft laughter following him. She's laughing. That's good, isn't it? He stuck his head around the kitchen door and heaved a sigh of relief.

"Oh thank God. Would you mind waiting in here? Please?"

Meaghan stood up, dusted off her knees, and almost had her smile under control by the time she reached the kitchen door. When she saw the room beyond she smirked at him.

"You're leaving me in the kitchen?"

"Just for a second!"

Meaghan's shoulders shook with silent laughter as he pulled out a chair for her at the kitchen table.

"I'll be back in a minute," he reassured her, then darted back to the front door where he'd left the bags of leftovers. "One more minute!" he promised, depositing the bags on the counter and running off again.

Idiot, he berated himself. He'd invited Meaghan in from his freezing doorstep to an equally freezing cottage that looked like a whirlwind had been through it.

His cottage.

A lump of cold settled in the bottom of his stomach. Meaghan was here, in the closest thing he had to a home, and this was the welcome he gave her? It was unacceptable.

Caine righted the last cushion and was halfway back to the kitchen when he looked down and saw muddy footsteps on the tiled floor. Cursing, he looked around for a vacuum cleaner.

No luck. He grabbed the throw rug he'd rescued from the staircase and dragged it over the dirt, sweeping some of it out to the front door.

Something that sounded suspiciously like muffled laughter echoed out from the kitchen.

"One more minute!" he called.

83

Caine dragged off his twinkling boots and left them on a low shelf next to the front door which must exist for that specific purpose, given that Meaghan's boots were already neatly lined up on it. But he couldn't just leave the dirt-streaked rug by the door. Casting around, he spotted a cupboard and opened it to find…

… a vacuum cleaner.

Caine groaned and knocked his forehead against the cupboard door as he closed it.

Everything had been going so well. He'd never forget the look in Meaghan's eyes when he told her how much he wanted her.

And now his demon hound had risen from the grave to ruin things again. And he hadn't even noticed until it was too late. He'd been sleepwalking through his first day as a free man.

"Caine? Your minute's up."

Caine closed his eyes. Meaghan's voice wound around his heart—but now he wasn't sure he deserved it. He was human again, but what sort of human? Meaghan was so sure in who she was. So brilliantly, fiercely herself. But Caine wasn't the man he had been before the demon. He didn't know who he was now.

The sort of man who didn't even notice the mess he caused and made her frightened that his home had been invaded. The sort of man who tracked dirt into his own house. Who forgot his wallet.

A bitter taste flooded his mouth. If he'd been sleeping before, this was a harsh wakeup call.

What if he wasn't enough for her?

What if he got the all of Meaghan's all-or-nothing heart, and didn't deserve it?

He walked slowly back to the kitchen and paused with his hand on the door. Half of him expected to find Meaghan already standing on the other side, having decided that he wasn't worth the wait. His rental car was still around the side of the cottage, after all. He would more than deserve it if she decided to head back to town by herself. Or she could take the bed, tonight, and he'd curl up on the sofa.

He should tell her now. Let her know the option was there, at least.

Caine pushed the door open.

Meaghan was just where he'd left her, sitting at the kitchen table, looking out the window at the shadowy shape of the wood shed.

Just one thing had changed. There were two glasses of champagne on the table in front of her.

CHAPTER TEN

Meaghan

All or nothing. That's how she dealt with everything, wasn't it? And Caine had been clear that he didn't want to be nothing.

And she didn't, either.

So she'd grabbed the bottle of champagne out of the bag, hunted down some flutes—which hadn't been hard, the cottage was clearly meant to be a romantic getaway even if Caine had been treating it more like a teenage boy's rec room, emphasis on the "wreck"—and now here she was.

Caine hadn't said anything. He was just standing in the door, his blue eyes fixed on her, and Meaghan had to clamp her hands on the edge of the table to stop herself from grabbing both glasses and swigging them down. All or nothing could mean *all* the champagne for herself, right? And, ideally, passing out immediately.

Except that would probably require more than two glasses of champagne.

Maybe I should jump out the window and hide in the wood shed until he forgets I was ever here.

"I hope one of those is for me." Caine's voice was soft, with deep undercurrents that caught at Meaghan's heart.

Or maybe not.

Meaghan let out a short breath and with it, all the tension that had been building up in her neck and shoulders. She picked up both glasses and walked over to Caine, feeling slightly light-headed.

"That depends. Is it safe to go out there again?"

Caine winced. Adorably. Meaghan's heart fluttered. "Just don't look in the hall cupboard."

"You even remembered to take your shoes off this time."

"I learn. Slowly." He took one of the glasses. "Just to check: shoes off for houses, but leave them on in restaurants and shops?"

"Scrape the soles off before you go in, but yeah, most places around here have wood or concrete floors so they can mop up the mess. Speaking of scraping, what were you doing out there?"

Caine's cheeks went faintly pink. "Ah. Trying to wipe up some of the dirt I tracked in earlier."

She waited.

"With a rug." Caine groaned. "Why am I telling you this?"

"Don't they have vacuum cleaners in the city?" Meaghan teased. He groaned again, his throat bobbing in a way that made Meaghan's insides tighten.

She raised her glass hurriedly. "Cheers."

"Cheers," Caine echoed, and clinked his glass against hers.

They were as close as they had been when she grabbed him under the trees that afternoon. She'd been red-hot with righteous rage, so turned-around and upset her head had felt like it was about to explode, and now…

Now, she was red-hot for another reason. And if her head was about to explode it would be from nerves and anxiety and—and—

Caine was watching her expectantly. Flustered, Meaghan took a sip of champagne. The bubbles hit the soon-to-explode feeling in her brain… and melted it away.

"To kidnappings gone wrong," she toasted, and took another sip.

Caine laughed. "To kidnappings gone very, very right," he retorted, and this time, Meaghan's full smile escaped before she could rein it in. "If I keep saying it, maybe one day I'll convince you," he proclaimed.

One day, Meaghan thought. She tucked the words away in her heart.

"Good luck with that," she said out loud, clinking her glass against his again.

"Thank you. I expect I'll need it."

"Hey!"

Caine grinned at her, and then his expression softened. The way he was looking at her… no one ever looked at her like that.

"Meaghan," he murmured, "today has been… Words can't describe it."

The tight, hot sensation inside Meaghan flared. "Crazy?" she said.

Some part of her still didn't believe this was really possible. *Turn it into a joke and you won't get hurt.*

"The best sort of crazy." Caine shook his head.

"Miserably cold and uncomfortable."

"Once I got out of the dog box, things improved." Caine gazed at her from under lowered eyelids, but there was a hint of mischief in his warm, inviting look.

Meaghan licked her lips. "Frustrating."

"…In some ways."

Oh God. She couldn't endure this for another second.

Meaghan wrapped her arms around Caine's shoulders. The heat of his skin burned through his too-small shirt. His hands found her waist, strong and hard. His face was less than an inch from hers.

She hesitated for one heartbeat, and then Caine moaned something wordless and pulled her closer and she pressed her lips against his.

The kiss made her skin thrill. An electric pulse shot from her lips to between her legs, shocking her with her own sudden need. Then Caine's lips were moving against hers with more wordless murmurs, and his tongue slipped out.

Meaghan gasped. Caine was pressed close against her. She'd never kissed anyone her own height before. They fit together like they were made to do this, her curves melting against his hard muscles. She wound her arms around him, reaching up to run her fingers through his hair.

It was perfect. Wonderful. The best—

"Ow!" Meaghan hissed with pain as a muscle in her shoulder spasmed.

"What's wrong?" Caine's hold on her turned from strong and needing to delicate in a second.

"My shoulder—*ow*. My neck." Meaghan lowered her head carefully, wincing. "It's just a cramp. It'll be gone in a minute." *As soon as the mood is totally ruined.*

Caine ran his fingers gently down her neck and moved on to her shoulders. Meaghan barely managed to bite back a moan. "You're so tense."

"It's been a long day." Meaghan winced again and closed her eyes. "Week. Month. *Months.*"

"Since Halloween?" Caine lifted her chin with one finger and Meaghan opened her eyes. "I have an idea that might help with that."

"It just needs a bit of heat and—"

"A massage?"

Caine's voice did *things* to her. Meaghan took a deep breath.

"That would be... nice."

Caine's eyes looked hot. They shimmered, like the air above a hot sidewalk in the summer.

"It's still freezing in here," he said, his voice achingly enticing. "It won't warm up for ages yet. But it's a beautiful night, and there's a hot tub on the balcony upstairs."

*

Meaghan stepped out onto the balcony, wrapped in a huge fluffy gown that had been hanging up in the master bedroom.

Caine had showered first and she'd followed, because the last thing either of them wanted was to clog up the hot tub with dog hairs. Meaghan had spent most of her shower straining her ears through the roar of the water. Her breath had shivered as she heard Caine's footsteps on the stairs, and moving through the master bedroom. The click of the balcony door.

She had almost managed to convince herself that her breath was hitching from the pain in her neck until she walked through the balcony door. She stared at the clouds of steam rising from the hot tub.

And at Caine.

He was sitting with his arms out over the sides of the cedar-wood tub. Water lapped at his chest. Steam wreathed around him and gathered in tiny drips on his skin.

It must have been the heat that was finally banishing the sick, pale look from his cheeks. His lips were red and hot-looking against the dark shadow of his stubble.

Meaghan felt hot, too, a sweet, liquid heat that poured through her veins, pooling low in her belly and between her legs.

This is really happening, she thought, licking her lips and remembering the feeling of Caine's lips pressed against them.

All or nothing.

"Close your eyes," she demanded, and Caine's eyes snapped shut. Meaghan took a deep breath.

Argh, it's cold. He's going to open his eyes again and I won't even have made it to the tub. I'll be standing right here, a full-body popsicle.

She took one tentative step forward, then another, careful to close the door behind her. Caine's eyebrows twitched as it clicked closed, but he didn't open his eyes.

One more step took Meaghan to the edge of the hot tub.

She stopped again, long enough to convince herself that his eyes really were closed… and just to look at him.

Every time she took her eyes off him, part of her thought, *No, surely* **he's not as mind-numbingly gorgeous as you remember him being**, and then when she was looking at him, he was so distractingly charming and annoying that she could almost ignore his looks.

Now, she was absolutely proving to herself just how unbelievably handsome Caine was.

Her breath caught in her throat. Mind-numbingly stunning, yes, but that wasn't all. Sitting there with his eyes closed, Caine looked like she'd never seen him before. Almost… vulnerable. She could see all the fine lines around his eyes, the delicate pulse in his temple. The dark shadows around his eyes that told of interrupted sleep and long-term exhaustion.

And the expression on his face, patient, still… and hopeful.

Meaghan squeezed her own eyes shut, dropped the robe, and stepped slowly into the hot tub.

Hot water enclosed her. She could feel every ache and pain

and knotted muscle in her body start to ease as heat hugged her limbs. Meaghan sat back, resting against the smooth wooden side of the tub, and a slight moan escaped her lips.

"Can I open my eyes yet?" Caine breathed.

Meaghan glanced down. The water covered her breasts… but it was just water. Water, that famously transparent liquid.

It's not like you're the only one who's stripped naked, she told herself. *You're naked. He's naked. That's fair, right?*

Unlike earlier, when he was mostly naked and you were wrapped up in your snow gear. Really, to be fair, you should be the one who—

She cut that thought off sharply, and not just because the moment her brain had thought the words '*he's naked*' her gaze had started slipping downwards.

Well, that's a relief. The light from the bedroom was reflecting off the water, and combined with the dark night, everything beneath the surface was hidden in shadows.

"You can open your eyes," she said, and a tingle of excitement went up her spine.

Caine's eyelashes fluttered. His eyes glinted, the irises almost swallowed by the deep black of his pupils. And he didn't immediately smirk, or make a nasty remark about her broad shoulders or stretch marks, or leer at her chest… he looked at *her.* Straight into her eyes.

So she kissed him again.

Her kiss before had been brash, like leaping off a cliff without looking. This one was more careful, even though she knew there were no rocks waiting for her below. She wanted to do this right; she wanted to explore every movement of his lips and tongue. She slid one hand up to rest on his cheek and brushed her thumb against his dark stubble.

By the time their lips parted, she was panting. Caine rested his forehead against hers.

"Turn around," he murmured.

"What?"

"Your neck's still cramped." His hand came to rest on the knot she'd been trying not to strain. "I told you, you need a massage."

Meaghan turned around slowly.

"Rest your head on your arm. Like that. So you're not tensing up."

Meaghan did as Caine said, lying her arm on the side of the tub and resting her forehead on it. She let out a slow breath. "This already feels better."

"Just wait."

Caine started on her shoulders, gently at first, then pressing his thumb into the knottiest muscles and slowly, determinedly massaging them out. By the time he reached the twanging muscle in her neck, Meaghan felt like she was melting into the water.

"Watch out," she murmured urgently as his fingers swept towards the sore spot. "That's—"

"I know." Caine slowed down. "It needs special attention." His fingers smoothed over the tight muscle, gently easing it. Meaghan sighed. "Is this from dog-sledding?"

"No. Old injury. Never really came right."

"What did you do?"

Well, he might as well know what he's getting himself into. "Threw myself off a wall trying to keep up with the cool kids. Broke my ankle, but no one noticed the whiplash until my neck seized up so much I couldn't turn my head."

"I guess going all-or-nothing doesn't always work out."

Meaghan snorted. She braced herself for a jolt of pain, but it didn't come. "I'd say it has about a ninety-five per cent strike rate, yeah."

Caine's fingers paused. She felt his breath on the back of her neck, somehow hotter than the warm vapor whirling above the water.

"Seems like a lot of risk for a small chance of reward."

Meaghan's shoulders tensed. She breathed deep, forcing them to relax.

"I do it because the rewards are always worth it," she lied. "Especially—*mmf*."

Caine chuckled. "That got it?"

His hands lifted from Meaghan's shoulders and she straightened up, stretching her neck and shoulders tentatively.

"That feels so much better. You're a miracle-worker."

Caine smiled smugly. "I may be a mannerless city slicker who doesn't know to take his shoes off inside, but I am good for some things."

Meaghan's mind immediately leapt to some of the things he might be good at. A shiver of ridiculous excitement prickled across her skin. "Really?"

"Want another demonstration?"

Meaghan was almost panting. "Yes."

Caine took her face in his hands and kissed her again.

Meaghan melted into his touch. Kissing Caine was everything a kiss should be. His lips were soft and warm, the scratchy stubble around them a delicious contrast. She kissed him harder.

She knew the rewards weren't worth the risk. They never were. But that didn't stop her. It *couldn't* stop her. Not even now.

Sorry, future Meaghan. She was riding a reckless wave of impulse and it had to break sometime, but if she was going to look back on this and hate herself then she was going to hate herself for the best damn kiss in the universe.

Meaghan pulled back to breathe, only far enough that their

lips just parted, and Caine made a noise that tugged at her insides as he crushed her against him, the warmth of his lips turning to fire, his hands hot on her skin, and the wave was crashing down around her and—

"I've wanted to hold you like this since the moment I saw you," Caine murmured against her lips.

Meaghan was soaring. The wave had broken, and she was flying far above it.

"Hmph," she said. "I had different things on my mind."

Caine chuckled silently, his shoulders shaking under her hands. "Like worrying about me passing out from hypothermia and the crippling weight of my own idiocy?"

He brushed his lips along Meaghan's jawline. She closed her eyes, her breath catching as he bit gently down on her earlobe.

"I thought the universe must be playing some sort of joke. I finally track down the guy who'd been causing so much trouble and he turns out to be a gorgeous, half-naked man." Meaghan tried to make it sound like a grumble, but her voice kept hitching as Caine's kisses grazed down her neck. "And then you kept being so *nice*... I thought it had to be a trick."

"I thought you hated me." Caine kissed her collarbone.

"I hated how goddamn *gorgeous* you were. And how you kept being helpful when I was acting like you were the spawn of Satan. And how much the dogs liked you. And—"

Meaghan's heart began to pound. *Stop talking stop talking stop talking.*

"—and when it turned out I'd gotten it all wrong and you didn't run for the hills, I thought you had to be sticking around to get back at me somehow and—"

Caine cut her off with a kiss. When he spoke there was a protective growl in his voice.

"I stuck around because I wanted to spend more time with you." His tongue teased her lower lip. "I would have admitted to being the whole ghost gang if I thought it meant you'd keep me tied up in your truck."

Laughter bubbled out of her. "You'd have been tied up in Jackson's truck, not mine."

"Nope." Caine slipped one hand behind her head as he kissed her again, slowly and gently. "I would have run out of there, set a false trail to put the rest of them off the scent, and waited for you to find me."

"Because I would have raced after you, even if the police were already on it?"

"No doubt." Caine smiled conspiratorially. "And you would have done a better job of it."

Meaghan half-groaned, half-sighed. "Again. No one's going to thank you for *encouraging* me to always be throwing myself into other people's business."

"They're lucky to have you around." Caine's voice dropped. "*I'm* lucky. Lucky you dragged me back to town and lucky you didn't throw me out on my ass when you had to pay for dinner. And extremely lucky that your truck broke down."

He took Meaghan's hand. "I've had too much—work—breathing down my neck this year. Hell, I'm here, alone in the most festive town in America, at Christmas, because of a—a project." His fingers tightened around hers, jerkily, as though they were reflecting his hesitant voice. "It took being kidnapped by a gorgeous woman to make me realize what I've been missing out on."

Meaghan's heart pounded so hard she was sure her whole body must be shaking. Caine's eyes were burning into hers through the white vapor of their mingled breath and the steam coming off the water. The expression in them warmed her deep inside.

96

"I, um," she said, her tongue tripping over feelings she couldn't put words to. "I don't have any Christmas plans, either?"

Caine's expression cleared. Something like firelight danced in his eyes, and then he put his hands on either side of her face and kissed her. Water sloshed over the sides of the tub, but Meaghan hardly noticed. There were more important things to pay attention too. Like his lips. And the teasing flicker of his tongue. And his hands. And the things he was doing with his hands. Holding her. Caressing her. Sliding down…

Meaghan lost her balance. There was a moment of splashing, and water up her nose, and then Caine's arms were around her. He pulled her up, crushing her against his chest.

And other parts of his anatomy.

"Sorry," he said, his voice rough. "If I'm moving too fast…"

Meaghan caught her breath. Droplets of water beaded on her eyelashes, splitting the light into rainbows that lit up the shadows of the balcony. She blinked, and the world spun into focus again.

Her breasts were pressed against Caine's chest. When she breathed, her nipples brushed against him. Lower, his abs were hard against the rounded softness of her own belly, and something even harder was jutting against her hip.

Meaghan licked her lips. Caine's eyes tracked the movement, and she got the impression that if his voice hadn't already trailed off, that would have sent it completely off-track. Her insides shivered with excitement.

"I don't want to slow down," she said, and Caine's eyes went pitch black with desire. "But maybe we should get out of the tub before you try that again."

He stood up with her in his arms so quickly that all the breath left her lungs. She didn't even have time to worry about him seeing her body before he'd leapt—actually *leapt*, that couldn't be safe—out of the tub. He landed on the balcony with animal grace and before Meaghan could so much as draw breath to complain about the cold, whipped her inside and closed the door behind them.

"That—" Meaghan wrapped her arms around herself as Caine set her on her feet. "—was—" He darted away, and she turned to follow him just as he reappeared, carrying a fluffy towel. "—*wow*."

Caine wrapped the towel around her and pulled her close for a kiss. Meaghan laughed.

"When I said I didn't want you to slow down, I wasn't meaning to go *superhuman* fast," she joked.

A shadow passed across Caine's face. "Super—?" he began, then shook his head. "I didn't mean to scare you."

"You didn't scare me." Meaghan shuffled closer to him. "If I'd had to haul myself out of that tub, I'd have frozen solid before I got halfway across the balcony."

"It's hardly warmer in here." Caine frowned and ran the back of his hand over Meaghan's arm. Despite the heat pooling inside her, her skin had goose bumps. "I can check the thermostat—"

"No." Meaghan was still soaring, but that was the problem with flying: the longer you stayed up, the further there was to fall. She shoved the thought away. *Maybe this time the risk will be worth it.* "Can't you warm me up right here?"

A wicked smile crept onto Caine's face. "I can certainly try."

He tipped her head back and kissed her, then moved down her neck, teasing her with his lips until she thought her legs would give out.

One hand behind her head, the other around her waist, he led her slowly backwards until she bumped into the bed.

"May I?"

Meaghan almost laughed. He was the one who'd wrapped her

up in the towel—*after* picking her up butt-naked and carrying her in here—and he was asking her permission to take it off her again? Then she looked into his eyes and her laughter turned into a gulp of fluttering nerves.

"Please," she whispered.

Caine unwrapped her carefully, like she might break if he touched her too hard. The opposite was true. Every light brush of his fingers against her skin sent tremors through her.

If he even breathes on me now I think I'll crack into a thousand pieces, she thought as Caine pulled the towel away from her body.

"You're gorgeous," he said, his eyes black as night.

Meaghan wriggled, her shoulders driving up towards her ears. Caine's gaze sharpened. He put one finger over her lips just as she opened them.

"Don't argue." His voice was firm, but the corner of his mouth curled up. "Not about this. You won't win."

Meaghan shut her mouth. Caine kept his finger pressed to her lips as he ran the towel over her arms one at a time.

"You won't warm up if you're all wet," he explained, dragging the towel down her back. She shivered and he smirked, replacing his finger on her lips with his own mouth. "Not that sort of wet, anyway."

"Hey!" Meaghan yelped. He laughed, his teeth bumping against hers, and the shivery-breaky feeling inside her exploded into a need that was stronger and more full of joy than anything she'd felt for anyone in her life. "Rude," she gasped as he knelt, drying her legs. "You're the one who's still soaking wet."

Caine's back was glistening with water. Rivulets ran down his chest as he straightened. "Am I?"

"So much for warm and dry." Meaghan traced a pattern through the droplets on Caine's chest, and he shivered. "You're freezing. Again." Except he wasn't really; his skin was furnace-hot.

"I guess there's something about you that makes me forget about the cold." Caine tipped her slowly back onto the bed.

Meaghan laughed as water dripped from his chest onto her. Caine pulled the towel up to dry her off again and she wrestled it off him, slung it around his shoulders and then somehow he was kissing her again and forget the towel, she wanted to touch him the way he was touching her, like she'd die if every inch of her wasn't touching every inch of him…

They broke apart, both gasping for breath. Meaghan's mouth felt bruised. The rest of her was a throbbing pulse of *want.*

Oh, shit.

Caine rolled on top of her, cupping her face in his hands. He kissed her, almost long enough for her to forget what she'd just realized, but when he lifted his head again she couldn't stop herself from grimacing.

"I'm not on anything," she explained.

"Not on—?" Caine's look of confusion faded and he groaned. "And I didn't exactly come prepared for anything like this."

"Really?" Meaghan's eyebrows shot up.

"I've had other things on my mind." Caine groaned again, burying his head in her shoulder. "Of course, at the moment I have *nothing else* on my mind…"

The hot weight of his cock pressing into Meaghan's thigh was evidence of that. She bit down on her lower lip as her core throbbed with need.

She'd never expected things to get this far. But now that they had…

"All or nothing, right?" she muttered.

"*Meaghan.*" Caine propped himself up on his elbows and gazed down at her, desire and humor mingling in his gaze. "Tomorrow

I'll go shopping. Tonight... I have a better idea."

He moved slowly down her body, kissing and grazing his teeth over her skin until she was writhing with anticipation. When he finally dipped between her legs she almost screamed.

Caine lifted his head. "What was that?"

"Don't stop!" Meaghan gasped. "I—mmf!"

Stars exploded behind her eyes. She gave up on speaking and let her head hang back. Caine was—*incredible.* There was no other word for it. This, what he was doing, was *actually happening* and she could still hardly believe it. His tongue—his fingers—

Pleasure spiraled into a sudden sharp jolt of sensation inside her and Meaghan cried out, her legs kicking automatically. Caine mumbled something, and even though she couldn't make out the words, his voice sent shockwaves up her spine.

"What?" Meaghan raised her head and immediately regretted it. The sight of Caine between her legs—*her legs*—was almost enough to make her brain explode.

Caine kissed her inner thigh. "Is kicking me off your way of telling me to slow down?"

"Never." Meaghan looped one leg over his shoulders, amazed at herself. "The opposite."

Caine's grin was wolfish. He lowered his head and Meaghan gasped as he slid his fingers into her. He kissed her and his tongue flicked out, circling her clit, drawing out ribbons of pleasure that wound together, tighter and tighter until her whole body was a taut cord of anticipation.

He's so good at this, Meaghan thought, fighting her body's need to writhe helplessly as Caine pleasured her. *It's like he knows every spot that—oh-h-h—*

Meaghan gasped as Caine curled his fingers inside her. She pushed herself up until she could see him and something about the sight of him so intent on pleasing her pushed her over the edge.

Her whole body tightened as pleasure exploded through her, a lightning blast with aftershocks that left her panting and weak. Her foot dug down into Caine's back as she twisted, but he didn't let her move. He kept her locked in place, licking and stroking her until she was too dizzy with orgasm to think straight.

Caine kissed his way back up her trembling body and lay beside her. Meaghan curled into his side, her head spinning.

Her whole body felt… right. Like this was exactly where she was meant to be. She ran one hand up Caine's chest, losing herself in how firm his muscles were, and the heavy thud of his heartbeat.

Caine caught her wandering hand and gently bit her fingertips.

Even through her happy fog, Meaghan felt desire tighten inside her. She pulled her hand out of Caine's grasp… and let it slide downwards.

Caine's gasp as she took hold of his cock made Meaghan's soul sing. She tugged on it, gently, exploring its girth and weight… and length. The thought of having *that* inside her made her bones turn liquid.

"Oh God," Caine groaned as she tightened her grip. "Meaghan—"

She let go, trailing her fingers along his length. This slow, teasing exploration was unlike anything she'd ever done before. When she reached the base of his cock, she traced the outline of the deep V at the tops of his thighs, then laid her palm flat on his powerful quads. The muscle flexed under her touch.

She wasn't even touching his cock anymore but the knowledge that it was *there*, inches away from her fingertips, made her ache inside.

Meaghan slid her hand lower down Caine's thigh. Her

fingertips grazed a patch of rough raised skin like scar tissue.

Caine's hand closed around her wrist before she could explore any further. "Stop there," he muttered, his voice rough.

Meaghan stared at him, confused, and his cheeks went dark.

"I mean, you don't need to do that," he murmured after a moment. "If you do, I don't think I'd be able to stop myself wanting more."

"Me either," Meaghan admitted in a whisper. She waited for his response, not daring to breathe.

Caine rested his forehead against hers. "Tomorrow."

Meaghan sighed, but knew he was right. Caine kissed her and she kissed him back.

"Tonight has been perfect," Caine whispered against her lips. "Don't doubt that."

"And tomorrow will be even better?"

Caine chuckled and nuzzled under her ear. "Less crazy. Less frustrating. But just as wonderful. I promise."

Meaghan kissed him one more time, then lay down on Caine's shoulder. He kept his arms around her, holding her close as his breathing slowed.

Meaghan was exhausted, but she didn't fall asleep as easily.

She'd run. Jumped. Thrown herself all-in, like she always did. And things had turned out fine.

But she knew this was only the first hurdle.

Don't let me ruin this, she begged herself. *Don't push him too far. Don't make him end up hating you like everyone else in your life.*

CHAPTER ELEVEN

Caine

DECEMBER 21
(CHRISTMAS EVE EVE EVE EVE)

The first thing he was aware of was the warm weight of Meaghan's body curled into his. Her back was pressed against his chest and her shoulders were rising and falling with slow, steady breaths. His arm was draped over her and sometime in the night she'd taken his hand, tangling her fingers between his, and tucked it close against her chest.

Half asleep and more than half convinced he was dreaming, Caine tried to free his hand. One sleepy grumble from Meaghan stopped him in his tracks, and then her grumble turned into a contented sigh and she rolled onto her back, still holding onto his hand.

Caine's heart thudded. Yes, she was naked—*gloriously* naked, and holding his hand firmly between her incredible breasts—but that wasn't the reason his blood was singing in his veins. And the silence inside him, the blessed absence of the creature that had cursed his every step for the last year, wasn't the reason either.

She was in his bed. She'd slept here, warm and safe beside him, and even asleep she didn't want to let him go.

Meaghan was more than he'd ever dreamed of. More than he deserved. She was perfect.

See! I knew she was the one for us!

Cold sweat broke out on Caine's back. "Who said that?" he demanded.

Meaghan murmured sleepily, oblivious to the horror curling in Caine's gut. Whoever had spoken, it hadn't been out loud.

Whatever had spoken.

No—no, it can't be, not now—

Movement stirred in the shadows of his soul, and suddenly the creature was there, so close Caine could feel its thorny hairs pricking beneath his skin. He braced himself, but the attack he expected never came. The monster was back, but it wasn't trying to take form.

It was stiff-legged, trembling with restrained energy. Like a kid on Christmas morning. Caine's stomach churned.

Are you pleased now? The disembodied voice shivered with glee. *Our mate. Our* mate*! You were right. You caught her on your own. And now she's ours.*

Flames crackled at the edges of Caine's vision.

Caine felt sick. How could he have been so careless? The monster wasn't gone. It had just been waiting. Lurking out of sight until...

Meaghan.

I stayed out of the way! Secret. Stealthy. And you won her! The monster leapt with excitement, and Caine's arms jerked with the movement. Smoke poured from his skin. *And now she's ours!*

"No!"

"Caine?"

Meaghan's eyes fluttered open. Her gaze was fuzzy with sleep, eyelids heavy, lips turning up in a lazy smile.

Our mate!

Caine wrenched his hand away, and the sleepy warmth in Meaghan's eyes sharpened.

"What's wrong?" She sat up.

Caine backed off the bed, almost tripping over the sheets in his hurry. "Nothing's wrong," he said quickly, and the sharpness in Meaghan's eyes turned hard. She pulled the blankets up over herself.

"Nothing's wrong," Caine repeated, the lie clanging in his ears. "I just have to—"

His throat went dry. *Leave. Run.* It was the truth, but he couldn't say it, not without making the hard look in Meaghan's eyes shatter.

He had to go. It was the only way he could protect her.

Protect her? We will protect her! She is our mate!

The monster's voice thundered against Caine's skull. He winced, gripping the doorframe.

Meaghan's eyebrows drew together. "Well, good morning to you, too."

"I wish it was." The words were out before he could stop them. Meaghan's face dropped. "Meaghan, I—"

A crash on the roof interrupted him. Meaghan looked up, eyes wide, and Caine was beside her at once.

Whatever had landed on the roof had been heavy. Big.

"What the hell was that?" Meaghan's head whipped around as something scraped across the roof and another crash echoed from outside. "That sounded like metal. Isn't your car out there?"

Alarms went off in Caine's mind. If whoever, or whatever, was out there had targeted his car, then they were trying to cut off his means of escape.

His chest clenched. Not *his* means of escape. *Theirs.*

Meaghan was in danger, and that was more important than any risk to his own safety.

Protect her! the monster screamed inside his head.

Meaghan scrambled out of the bed and ran to the balcony window, wrapping a blanket around herself. "Holy crap," she muttered.

Caine's instincts screamed at him to get her away from the window. He reached out to pull her back towards the bed, but by the time he crossed the room she'd already darted away. The bathroom door swung behind her.

"What are you doing?"

She reappeared around the door, dragging her sweater over her head. "I'm going out there."

"Let me check it out first," Caine argued, and she stuck out her chin.

He cast around the floor for his own clothes and threw them on as Meaghan pulled up her pants. The obstinate look on her face did not bode well for his skills of persuasion.

"If it's the ghost gang—" *They're not human. They're not* safe. The words stuck to the roof of his mouth.

"You're not going to stop me going out there." Meaghan drew herself up.

Caine's chest ached. The pain in Meaghan's eyes was like a knife between his ribs. And it was all his fault.

Because the first thing she saw when she woke up was me running away from her.

His body felt heavy, weighed down by the knowledge that he was only going to hurt her more. His demon wasn't gone; it had tricked him. And that meant he was going to keep running away from Meaghan. It was the only way to keep her safe.

"I'm going down there." Meaghan's eyes were shining, with tears as well as determination. She pointed out the window. "And you are too, because if it is the ghost gang then I need you to tell me I haven't completely lost it. Because whatever did *that* to your car? Isn't human."

Caine stared out the window. His rental car was just visible, tucked down beside the woodshed.

Huge gouges had been taken out of its top and trunk. The sorts of marks that could only be made by giant claws.

A chill seeped through his veins. The suspicion that had twisted in the back of his mind ever since he heard about the ghost gang grew stronger.

The gang were monsters.

Like him.

He had to tell her.

Throat raw, Caine turned back—to an empty room.

"Meaghan! Don't go down there alone!"

Caine raced down the stairs. The front door slammed and he shoved it open just in time to see Meaghan stomping around the side of the house. He grabbed her arm and she stiffened as though electrified.

He let her go at once, hurt by her rejection and hurting more because he knew it was his own fault. All of this was his fault.

Meaghan shot him a wary glare, and then turned back to the car. "What could do something like that?"

"I—" Caine swallowed and forced himself to breathe. "Something big. With claws."

"How did it get on the roof?" Meaghan shaded her eyes as she looked up at the cottage, then around the clearing. "The trees aren't close enough to jump from. Could it…" Her eyes widened. "Honestly? After everything else, I wouldn't be surprised if whatever-it-is *can* fly."

"They can't." Caine's heart was heavy. *Just walk on the air like it's solid and move through walls like they're made of mist. An unstoppable, inescapable hunter.*

He gulped. "Meaghan, there's something I need to tell you. I should have told you before we—but I was a coward."

Meaghan's shoulders were up around her ears. She didn't look at him.

"I think it went in here," she said, as though he hadn't spoken.

Caine swayed. His head was pounding. He had to concentrate. If he lost his focus, even for a minute, then the monster would escape.

But Meaghan was already walking towards the wood shed, and whatever monster was waiting in there.

He ran past her, standing in front of the door. "Meaghan, please. Let me check it out first." The door was hanging from one hinge; whatever had hit it, had hit it *hard*.

Meaghan glared at him. "Let me through!"

"And what are you going to do if they're in there? Shout them into surrendering? That only works on me!"

Caine's instincts were screaming at him. They were on full alert and… doubled, somehow, or mirrored, two sets of sensory input and risk assessment reflecting and ricocheting off one another until he thought his skull would crack.

Then the storm broke. His pounding head was silent, except for an eerie sensation that the monster was laughing at him.

"What?" Meaghan searched his face. "What do you mean, that only works on you?"

"I—"

"Are you *joking* with me? You—first you act like you can't get away from me fast enough, and now you're *kidding around?*"

"Meaghan, I never meant—"

"Get out of my way!"

Caine stepped back automatically and Meaghan pushed past him. The door fell off its final hinge as she stormed through it. Caine knocked it out of the way. Thick hairs sprouted on his arms and for the briefest of seconds he paused—if Meaghan saw—but he had to protect her. And if the thing in the shed was what he thought it was, then being human wouldn't be enough.

But if it hurts her—

We would never *hurt our mate!* snarled the monster, just as Meaghan gasped.

"What on *earth?*"

Caine stepped in front of her, arms wide to ward it from whatever it was she'd seen. Meaghan made an irritated noise and ducked under his arm.

"Tell me I'm not going crazy," she said as Caine's eyes adjusted to the gloom inside the wood shed. "Tell me that isn't a *dragon.*"

CHAPTER TWELVE

Meaghan

I'm dreaming, Meaghan thought, and then her heart swooped miserably. *Yes, please, let this all be a dream and any minute now I'm going to wake up and do this whole morning over, without—without—*

"That's a dragon." Caine sounded as stunned as she felt.

Which meant this was real. Meaghan blinked. Which meant *dragons* were real.

And that Caine was so turned off by her that he'd tried to do a pre-dawn walk of shame from *his own house.*

One of those things is amazing. And the other really shouldn't come as a surprise. Meaghan swallowed hard and pinched herself.

"Ow."

"What happened?" Caine went stiff. He looked concerned, but... Meaghan swallowed again.

"Just... checking," she explained. "I'm definitely awake?"

"Afraid so." Caine's mouth quirked into that crooked half-smile that she'd found so addictive the previous night. Now it just made her feel sick.

Meaghan turned back to the dragon, blinking fiercely. When her vision cleared, it was still there.

The dragon was about twice the size of one of the Puppy Express huskies, covered in shiny black scales. Its wings were hunched up above its back and it was backing further into the shed, whipping its tail around like an angry cat. Brilliant blue eyes flicked from Meaghan to Caine and back.

"And that's definitely a dragon," she said weakly as it let out a puff of smoke and sparks. "Watch out!"

At her words, the dragon had jumped in the air and let loose another tiny fireball. Meaghan backed up, almost tripping over Caine as he tried to dive in front of her, and the dragon made a distressed cry and started stomping out the sparks that had landed on the wood shed floor. It stamped them all out and then looked up at her again, with an expression that looked exactly like the look Parkour got when he'd been caught trying to jump the fence again.

But—she couldn't be imagining this, could she?—there was far, far more intelligence behind those eyes than Parkour could dream of having.

"Thank you," she said automatically. "I appreciate you not trying to burn us to a crisp, little... dragon."

Beside her, Caine made a strange, vulnerable noise deep in his throat. But she didn't have time to figure that out, because the dragon was shivering—no, *shimmering*, like heat-waves were rising from every scale—and a moment later it had disappeared and there was a little boy sitting on the floor where it had been. Completely naked.

"No I'm not!" the boy insisted. "I'm not a dragon!"

"You're—" Caine began, his voice ragged.

"I'm not!"

"No, you're not." Meaghan said, pitching her voice over both the others. The little boy looked relieved. "You're Cole. Cole

Heartwell."

Cole's expression of relief vanished.

"Opal and Hank's little boy."

Cole looked nervous. "No-o-o, I'm—um…"

"You definitely are. I remember from when you came to the Grill last weekend with your parents. You ate fifteen donuts all by yourself."

"No! I ate *seventeen*!" Cole protested, and then shoved his hands over his mouth. "'m n't dr'gon!" he insisted, his voice muffled behind his hands.

Beside her, Caine made an exasperated noise, pulled his shirt off and handed it to the boy.

Meaghan's brain felt like it was on fire. She *knew* Cole. His parents took him to the Grill every weekend, probably because they were worried he'd eat them out of house and home otherwise. Cole was cheeky, and full of endless energy, and Hannah was probably going to ban him from all-you-can-eat when he reached his teens, but…

"You're Cole Heartwell and you can turn into a dragon," she whispered. Even saying the words didn't make them feel more real. "Dragons are real? And they live here? In Pine Valley?"

"Um-m-m…" Cole screwed up his face, as though he was hunting desperately for another explanation. He looked up at Caine as though he might find some help there, and Caine tensed.

Meaghan sank down onto her knees so that she was on Cole's level.

"Cole," she said gently. "Are you the one who landed on Caine's car?"

"No!" he retorted at once. She gave him her best *are-you-sure?* look and he wriggled uncomfortably, crossing his arms. Then inspiration struck and he threw them up, grinning. "I'm… I'm not the dragon! I'm *following* the dragon!"

Uh-huh. "And what about the ghost gang?"

"You're not meant to know that they're shifters!" Cole gasped and stuffed his hands into his mouth again, staring at her with his big blue eyes.

Meaghan felt as though she'd walked straight into a tree. Her head spun.

"Shifters? What's a shifter?"

"You're not supposed to know!"

Time seemed to stop. Meaghan stared at Cole, then looked up at Caine, and back at Cole. Understanding hollowed out a pit inside her.

She wasn't supposed to know that the people she'd labeled the 'ghost gang' were real. And this was why.

They weren't human.

"This is what everyone's been hiding from me," she breathed. "This is why everyone's been acting so weird lately."

"N-n…" Cole began. He hopped from foot to foot, staring imploringly at Caine. "N-n… yes?"

It made sense. It *all* made sense. No wonder Jackson had been so cagey about his investigation. And Bob had been so horrified when she came back claiming to have one of the gang in her trunk. And Olly had tried to reassure her that everything was fine, honestly, and don't bother chasing after…

After what? What had she been chasing down, when she went to rescue the dogs?

She groaned and rubbed her forehead. Too many thoughts. Too many questions. "So… the ghost gang are dragons?"

"No, they're not," Caine muttered under his breath. Meaghan frowned.

He didn't sound as amazed as she felt. For God's sake: *dragons.*

Everything she thought she knew about the world had just exploded in her face. So why did he sound like it was no big deal?

She backtracked, remembering what he'd tried to tell her before she stormed into the shed.

Meaghan, there's something you should know about me—

"No! But dragons are the most powerful shifters," Cole chirped. "That's why I... umm... the dragon went after them. And I was following the dragon to... to... umm..."

"Kid, there's no point trying to convince us we didn't just see you shift," Caine muttered, then sighed and rubbed his face. "And lying about this is... a bad idea. No. *No,* I'm not going to—"

He caught Meaghan staring at him and broke off. Meaghan stood up. *That sounded like he was talking to someone else. What the hell is going on here?*

Caine's been lying to me, too?

Meaghan squeezed her eyes shut. When she opened them, they were clear. She stood up.

"Right. Here's what's going to happen. Cole, you're a dragon. *Don't* try to tell me you're not. I saw you, and anyway, there's no way you would have gotten all the way down here from Heartwell Lodge with no clothes on without freezing your butt off."

"What if I rode that dragon?" Cole suggested.

"Cole, I just *saw* the dragon. Who is you. And that dragon was *not* big enough for anyone to ride on."

Cole scuffed his foot on the singed floor. "Oh, fi-i-ine. I am the dragon then."

"Does your mother know you're out here?"

Cole eyes flicked side to side. "...Yes?"

He grinned hopefully, and Meaghan gave him a *look.*

"Guess what? I don't believe you. So we're all going to go back inside, and I'm going to call your parents and—" Meaghan braced herself with a deep breath. "—and Caine, *you* are going to—what's wrong?"

Caine was clutching his head. "Headache," he gritted out from between clenched teeth. "Too loud—can't—*stop it*—"

Meaghan stepped towards him automatically. If he was hurting, she wanted to help. Then a shadow fell across the open shed door, as though the morning sun had just gone behind a cloud.

"Umm," Cole said, jumping from foot to foot again, "You have to tell them I wasn't chasing the ghost gang! I just got lost!"

"Tell who?" Meaghan asked, bewildered.

Caine staggered out the door. Meaghan followed him and gasped.

Three massive dragons were flying above the cottage.

CHAPTER THIRTEEN

Caine

Dragons. Christ almighty.

Caine had heard of them, of course; he'd come to Pine Valley seeking one. He had thought he was prepared for it.

He'd been wrong.

They were huge. The nearest was a bold forest green color. It was flying so close to the ground that the pines around Caine's cottage swayed and lost their snow when it flapped its wings.

The second dragon, flying just above it, had a more sinuous body and pale, opalescent scales. Finally, wheeling above them like a firestorm, was a huge red dragon with wings like a burning sunset. It was clutching something against its chest with one foreclaw.

A shaft of pain crashed through Caine's temple. He staggered, clutching his head. With whatever was assaulting his brain from the outside, and the demon howling inside, his skull felt as though it was about to shatter.

"Caine!" Meaghan grabbed his arm. He leaned into her gratefully—then remembered himself.

He pulled out of her grip, trying not to see the hurt that flashed across her face. "No. Can't—risk it," he muttered, a reminder to himself. Meaghan would only be hurt more if he weakened now.

Another bolt of pain. He looked around, eyes watering, and found Cole staring at him. The boy frowned.

"Mom! Dad! He can't hear you!" Cole shouted, using his hands as a loudspeaker. The green dragon cracked its wings with a sound like thunder. "No-o-o, he's not one of *them*! Yes I'm fine!"

Caine rubbed his temple. The sudden migraine was fading, but there was a strange... echo around each of Cole's words. As though he was hearing them *inside* his head as well as outside.

"But you told me it was *polite* to talk out loud when I'm around humans! Like Auntie Abigail!" Cole bawled at the circling dragons.

This time, Caine was ready for the pain.

It's a conversation, he realized. *A conversation between people beating on my skull like a drum.*

Despite the thudding in his head, Caine managed a smile. Meaghan would find that funny. She—

Caine glanced across at her and his stomach went cold. "Hey!" he called out, and then louder, his face to the sky, "Hey! Dragons!"

The dragons' sudden attention hit him like a punch. He braced himself.

"Stop flying around like that!" His voice was gravelly. "You're disturbing Meaghan."

The clamor in his head stopped. Caine breathed a sigh of relief. He turned to Meaghan.

She'd been ashen when he glanced at her, her dark skin washed with gray and her mouth in a thin unhappy line. Caine ran his hands through his hair to stop himself from taking her in his arms.

"It's okay," he said. "They don't mean any harm."

"I figured that much," Meaghan snapped. "I can count, and I'm pretty sure I know who each of them is going to turn into when they land." She squeezed her eyes shut and took a deep breath, then glared at Caine. "They're not the ones *disturbing* me. Cole's acting like you're one of them. Saying you... should be able to hear something? Is this what you needed to tell me before?" she demanded. "Are you a dragon, too?"

Caine lowered his head. *I wish I was. That would make all of this so much simpler.*

"No. I'm—"

Meaghan had been glaring at him full-force, but something behind Caine caught her eyes. She took a half-step backward.

"Holy... wow."

The green dragon had landed. It folded its wings, almost taking the top off a nearby pine, and then shimmered and transformed into a sturdily-built man with red hair and a lumberjack beard.

"Cole, go let your mother see you're all right," the man said, and nodded to Meaghan. "Morning, Miss Markham. Thanks for looking after our runaway."

"Um," Meaghan said, as though her tongue was stumbling over real words. "Morning. Mr. Heartwell. Good to... see you..."

"Oh. Yes. 'Scuse me." Mr. Heartwell covered himself with his hands. "Left in a bit of a hurry. Don't worry. I'm sure someone will have remembered to bring some pants."

He looked Caine up and down. There was no aggression in his eyes, just a sense of careful observation that made Caine claw his monster back as deep as it would go.

"You must be the one to we have thank for the fact that my Cole isn't running around the snow ass-naked."

"Caine Guinness." Caine nodded a greeting.

"Hank Heartwell. Pleasure."

You say that now. Caine swallowed down a stomachful of bitterness.

The shimmering, opalescent dragon landed in front of Cole and wrapped him up in her wings before transforming into a dark-haired woman. Caine averted his eyes and saw Meaghan gaping at the woman.

"Opal? I mean, I figured, but… there's figuring and there's *seeing.*" She pressed the heels of her hands against her eyes. "I feel like my brain's about to explode."

"Why?" Cole popped up in front of her. "You don't have telepathy. Not even broken telepathy like him." He looked at Caine.

Meaghan lowered her hands and followed Cole's gaze. Her jaw set when she met Caine's eyes.

"Meaghan! Excuse the nakedness. I think Jasper's bringing Abigail and she's sure to have brought clothes." The dark-haired woman put her hands on Cole's shoulders and shooed him back to his father. "I'll hug you congratulations once we're all human-decent."

"Congratulations?" Meaghan frowned.

"You two! God, what good timing. Just in time for Christmas!" Opal grinned and looked up. "Hurry up, bro!"

"Christmas?" Meaghan was whispering, but her voice was as clear to Caine as if he'd been standing right beside her.

The final dragon soared out of the sky. It landed coiled around the cottage and carefully set down what it had been holding in its foreclaw: a woman in her mid-twenties, with a baby strapped to her front and a bag slung over her shoulder.

"Abigail?" Meaghan yelped. "Don't tell me you're a dragon, too?"

"No." Abigail petted her dragon on its massive front leg and walked up to Meaghan. She was the shortest person there, excluding Cole, with a curvy figure and blonde hair. Unlike everyone else who'd fallen out of the sky in the last five minutes, she was properly wrapped up against the cold.

She gave Meaghan a one-armed hug. "That's from Opal. And from me. Are you freaking out yet?"

"Freaking out about a load of dragons appearing in Pine Valley?" Meaghan's voice was weak. "Oh, no. This is a totally expected outcome to all the weird shit that's been happening lately. Dragons. Why not."

Abigail grabbed two bundles from her bag and threw them to Opal and Hank. Behind her, the final dragon shimmered and transformed into a dark-haired man with an athletic build and eyes that burned like hot coals.

Caine tensed, but—no. The fire in the dragon shifter's eyes was warm and protective, not the angry sparks that overflowed his own monster's eyes.

"Hi, Jasper," Meaghan called, sounding exhausted.

Three dragons. Caine straightened his shoulders. *Good.*

Cole was right. Dragons were among the most powerful shifters in the world. And these three were all Meaghan's friends. They would look after her.

Jasper strode up and put his arm around Abigail's shoulders. "Who's this?"

"Caine Guinness," Hank supplied.

"Jasper Heartwell. And you…" Jasper's voice had been light-hearted, but something flickered behind his eyes and his expression turned serious. "What *are* you? I can tell you're a shifter, but…"

Caine's demon rose up inside him. It clawed at his throat, scrambling to take form. Caine wrenched it back, but not before his eyes blazed with the demon's terrifying gaze.

It pinned Jasper with its—his—eyes. Jasper went pale, but whatever the demon was looking for, it didn't find it. Caine fought for control as the demon moved its attention to Hank, and then Opal. Each of them paled and stepped back.

Caine and the demon looked back at Jasper. Next to him. Abigail.

"Hey!" Jasper pulled Abigail closer to him. The protective gesture gave Caine the strength he needed to wrestle the demon back.

He never knew what would set off his demon's hunting instincts. If it ran wild now, with children around—and Meaghan watching—

His demon hound whined unhappily and Caine blinked. Jasper's protectiveness of his wife and child hadn't called up its worst instincts. The demon sounded—felt—lonely. It retreated so quickly Caine almost fell to his knees.

He's not for the hunt. None of them are. Meaghan—

Cold sweat broke out on Caine's forehead. *Stay away from her!* he howled at the creature.

"What the hell was that?" Meaghan's voice was sharp, but there was an edge of wonder in it that made Caine's heart ache. "Your eyes—I *knew* I hadn't imagined it. Yesterday, in the woods…"

Gasping, Caine raised his head. He couldn't look at her. Not when he knew that the wonder in her voice would soon turn to horror.

"Jasper Heartwell," he grated out. The dragon shifter flinched slightly as their eyes met, but his face didn't turn into the mask of terror it had when he faced the demon. "You're the shifter I've been hunting down since midyear."

No! Wrong!

Caine flinched. That wasn't a feeling. It was his demon's voice, splintering against the inside of his skull.

We shouldn't be hunting him. Why were we hunting him?

"I need your help," he gritted out over the demon's confusion. "Please. You Heartwells are the only shifters I've heard of who can get rid of their animal sides."

"Wait. What? Slow down." Meaghan stalked in front of him. She waved her arm at the Heartwells. "My neighbors are *dragons* and you—you *know* about them? And you're a shifter too, but you don't want to be?" She shook her head. "Why?"

She was close enough that he could have reached out and touched her. *She* was reaching out, her eyes full of innocent amazement—and he couldn't tell if the way his heart leapt at the sight of her was *his* reaction, or the creature's.

Ours, it whispered in his mind.

Caine clenched his jaw. He had to be strong. He'd made a terrible mistake, letting Meaghan into his life without knowing for sure that his demon was gone.

Had he really thought he could walk away from the nightmare he'd been living for the last twelve months? He should have known it would never stop chasing him.

And he needed to tell Meaghan the truth.

"Because you're right," he said. Meaghan's eyebrows shot together. "Everything that's happened to Pine Valley since Halloween isn't coincidence. The gang you've been chasing are shifters."

Meaghan nodded. "That's why no one would talk to me about it." Her eyes flicked around the rest of the group. "Bit late for that now, guys. Sorry."

Her eyes met Caine's again, and the trust in them made his shoulders heavy.

"So the ghost gang are real. Real shifters. Real, evil, scary shifters." She was getting angry again.

Good, Caine thought. His demon whined.

"Shifters who bring fear and terror wherever they go. Who terrorize innocent people." Caine took a deep breath. "The same sort of shifter as me."

"What?" Meaghan's eyes snapped to his. "But…"

Her face fell. The shock in her eyes made way for confusion. Caine tried to say something, anything, to reassure her, but his mouth wouldn't move.

"But you're not a monster," she said, her voice shaky.

"I don't want to be. That's why I'm in Pine Valley. The Heartwells are the only shifters I've heard of who can ever lose their animal sides." He turned to Jasper. "Please. Listen to me. I looked for you because I need your help. This—*thing*—inside me. I came here to ask you to help me destroy it."

He turned back to Meaghan as Jasper cursed under his breath. All three shifters looked horrified. Caine's head thudded. He took a deep breath, half expecting to breathe it out as smoke.

"Meaghan—I should have told you. I thought the monster was gone—that I'd gotten rid of it—but it was just hiding. Please believe me, I never would have gotten you involved in all of this if I thought it was still there."

Inside him, the creature's teeth ground together. It was pacing. Disturbed. Almost… scared?

It's dangerous, Caine reminded himself. Why else would every shifter he met be so terrified of it? Why else would the only other hellhound shifters he'd heard of be criminals? First the ones who'd done this to him, and now the ghost gang?

Criminals, the demon raged, *hurting the weak and unprotected. We must help her find them, hunt them, stop them—*

Them? Caine couldn't bear to look at Meaghan anymore. He

closed his eyes, turning his gaze inward to the fiery-eyed, smoke-wreathed monster wrapped around his soul. *She's talking about you. Us.*

We're the monster she hates so much.

The smoke that had been wreathing at the edges of his vision darkened. His demon hound clawed at him, dragging him into shadows so dark it was like light had never existed.

The last thing Caine saw before he lost consciousness was Meaghan's face.

CHAPTER FOURTEEN

Meaghan

"Caine!"

Meaghan leapt to catch Caine as he toppled forward. His body was completely limp and too heavy for her to hold. She lowered him as gently as she could, terror pulsing through her veins.

Oh God. Forget her own anger and confusion. None of that mattered. Not compared to the fear she felt when Caine collapsed. There had been one flare of smoky fire in the depths of his eyes, and then all the life had faded from his face.

She knelt over him. Caine was so pale his face looked gray. The purple shadows around his eyes looked like bruises. And he wasn't moving.

Meaghan glared up at Jasper. "What's happening? Is this some sort of shifter thing?"

It was Opal who answered. She'd wrapped the blanket Abigail had thrown her around herself like a toga, and her eyes were grave as she knelt down beside Caine's still body.

"Do you know how long it is since he last shifted?"

"I don't even know what that *means*!" Meaghan wailed. Even Caine's lips were losing their color. She touched his cheek, her fingers trembling. "Oh God. He's cold. *Really* cold."

Caine wasn't standing-in-the-snow cold. His skin had a chill that made Meaghan's breath catch. It was as though that furnace-heat inside him had gone out.

"Someone help me get him inside." Her voice buzzed in her ears, tinny and distant. "Help me!"

Hank and Jasper helped her carry Caine back into the cottage. They laid him down on the sofa and stepped back awkwardly as Meaghan stuck to his side like a magnet.

He was still cold. Too cold.

"Blankets upstairs," she barked. "Someone turn the thermostat up. And get the fire going. And then *get out.*"

Jasper cleared his throat. "Meaghan—"

Meaghan wasn't listening. Throat tight, she pressed her fingertips under Caine's jaw, trying not to think about how cold he was as she searched for his pulse.

Thud. Thud. Meaghan let out a breath that almost swelled into a sob.

"Go on, sweetheart," Abigail murmured. "I'll stay with her."

Meaghan was vaguely aware of the men leaving the room. Abigail settled down beside Meaghan and rested one hand on her shoulder.

"He'll be okay," she whispered. "Shifters are tough. Stupidly tough. Ask me how I found out about Jasper being a dragon one day."

"Dragons."

Meaghan swallowed. *Thud. Thud.* The icy panic in her own veins began to lose its edge. She took a shaky breath.

"All this… This is why Jackson and the rest of you kept telling me not to look into the ghost gang, isn't it? Because they're shifters. Like all of you are, and… and Caine."

His pulse flickered under her fingertips and she hissed in a breath, holding it until the beat steadied again.

Abigail sighed. "Yes. That was the plan. Pine Valley is a haven for the few shifter families who live here, and you're new in town, so… we thought it was the safest option."

"I thought I was going crazy." Not that that mattered, now. *Thud. Thud.*

"I'm sorry." Abigail squeezed her shoulder. "The safest option for us. Not so great for you."

The room was beginning to warm up. Caine's pulse was steady. He was breathing. Meaghan sat back, but kept one hand resting on his chest. Just in case.

"So why do it? Why not just tell me that, yes, there *was* something going on, and it was all under control?"

"Would that have stopped you trying to find them?"

Meaghan didn't even need to think about it.

"No." Her shoulders slumped. "All this time I've been trying to help and I've just been getting in the way."

Trust you, Meaghan. Fucking everything up. Going in like a bull in a china shop and smashing everything.

Abigail was shaking her head. "Like I said. Not such a great plan." She smiled over Meaghan's head. "Right, Opal?"

"Scared people make bad decisions." Opal sat down on Meaghan's other side. "And the ghost gang has everyone scared. Even us dragons. None of us have ever dealt with anything like these shifters before. Whoever the ghost gang are, they might as well be invisible. None of the local shifters can see, smell or sense them in any way, even when the Ghosts are chasing them. So when Cole telepathed me saying he'd found a shifter with no scent or psychic trace—"

"Caine isn't one of the ghost gang!" Meaghan snapped.

The bundle strapped to Abigail's front wriggled. One pudgy arm waved in the air, followed by a disgruntled gurgle.

Abigail's expression froze. Meaghan winced.

"Sorry," she mouthed.

"It's okay," Abigail said, and cooed at the baby. "What's up, Ruby? Did you have a good sleep?"

Six-month-old Ruby gurgled again. Happily.

Meaghan relaxed. She'd met Ruby a few times, and the baby had—she gulped—dragon-sized lungs.

She caught Opal's eyes. "Is she a shifter, too?" she whispered.

"She certainly *feels* like a shifter," Abigail grumbled. Which didn't really make things any clearer, from Meaghan's perspective.

"It'll be a few years before she shifts," Opal explained. "Her dragon's in there, but shifting takes a lot of energy, and right now she's using that energy to grow her human body."

Meaghan's mind was spinning. She leaned closer to Caine without realizing what she was doing. His heartbeat was reassuringly strong under her hand. "That... makes sense?"

Abigail gave her an understanding smile. "Don't bother trying to understand it all right now. Believe me. You'll give yourself a headache." She kissed Ruby on the top of her head. "I don't even understand all of it yet. Especially with bub here. Being the human mother of a shifter is... something." She exchanged a look with Opal.

Opal grinned. "You know, everything with you and Ruby should have tipped us off that there was stuff about shifters that we had no idea about, even before the ghost gang."

"Which Caine isn't involved with." Meaghan didn't know why she was so certain, except for—*All the evidence. Right? He's new in town. He wasn't with the guys that stole the dogs. Olly saw the ghost gang, and he isn't one of them.*

"I know." Opal held her hands up. "And I believe you."

"Ask Jackson if you don't believe me. He knows Caine had nothing to do with—" Meaghan's brain caught up with what her ears had just heard. "Oh."

"There is no way I would have brought bubs out here if I thought your boyfriend was an evil monster shifter," Abigail said reasonably as Ruby grabbed at her chin.

Meaghan looked down at Caine. Even unconscious, his face wasn't relaxed. There was a deep line between his eyebrows and as she watched, a muscle under his eye twitched. She held his hand tighter.

"That's what he thinks he is, though," she muttered. "A monster."

She closed her eyes and changed her grip on his hand so she could feel his pulse. Still there. Still strong.

"He's not my boyfriend, though," she said. "We only met yesterday and—uh..." *And hooked up a few hours later. And if Cole hadn't turned up, he would have dumped me in a hot minute.*

"And he hasn't told you anything," Opal muttered to herself. "*Men.* You'd better tell her, Abigail, you're the only one with experience on the human side of this. I'll let the boys know."

Meaghan watched Opal leave the room, her mouth hanging open. "Why do I feel even more crazy now than when I thought I was the only one who noticed what the ghost gang was doing?"

"Because shifters *are* crazy. Most of the ones I've met, anyway." Abigail sighed and settled herself more comfortably with her back against the sofa. "Jasper waited until he was almost dead before he told me about this, too."

"About what?"

Just then, Caine murmured something and Meaghan was on her feet at once. She leaned over him.

"Caine? Caine, can you hear me? What's wrong? Why won't you wake up?" Caine fell silent and Meaghan turned to Abigail. "We should call a doctor."

Abigail looked uncomfortable. "Not yet."

"What do you mean, not yet?" Meaghan hissed, so loudly that Ruby started to fuss again. Abigail sighed, and cradled her daughter until she quieted down again. "Are you all insane? I thought I was the crazy one, but none of you are making any sense! We need to call the clinic."

"No. And this is going to sound crazy, but…" Abigail cuddled Ruby and stared up at Meaghan, her eyes soft. "He doesn't need a doctor. He needs you."

Meaghan froze. "What the *hell* is that supposed to mean?"

"It means—look, you spent the night here, didn't you?"

"That's none of your business!" Meaghan yelped.

"All right. If you *did* spend the night here, and if you *do* feel like he's the most incredibly, ridiculously, completely irritating and yet somehow also completely wonderful man you've ever met…" Abigail's cheeks went pink. "…or maybe that was just me… but, anyway. If you feel like there's something special and scary between you that you've never felt before, then it's probably because you're his mate."

"His mate." Meaghan squeezed Caine's hand so hard his fingertips went white. She forced herself to loosen her grip, finger by finger, without letting him go.

The most incredible, ridiculously, completely wonderful man you've ever met—Okay, yes, maybe, but…

"What is that supposed to mean? I'm his friend? I only met him yesterday." Her voice fell. "I don't know anything about him." *I just think he's sexy, and funny, and now he's sick and I don't know what's going on and I can't let go of his hand…*

"But you know you want to be with him." Abigail's voice was warm and understanding. She wrapped her arms around Ruby. "All shifters have a mate. One person who's the other half of their soul, essentially. We—humans—talk about 'soul mates', but this is a bit more literal. Whatever Caine's animal is, it must have recognized you as his mate."

"That's why he ran away from me." Meaghan felt as though she'd wandered into a walk-in freezer and heard the door slam locked behind her. "That's why he was leaving. Because his shifter-thing wanted me, but he thinks it's a monster, so he thinks *I'm...*"

Her voice gave out at the same time as her knees did. She fell to the ground with a crack. Her eyes swam with sudden tears—*Because it hurts,* she told herself, and then fixed that to *Because my knees hurt*, because how freaking stupid would she have to be to be *hurt* by someone running off on a one-night stand—running away from her—thinking she was...

The other half of his monster's soul. Her mouth tasted bitter.

Run in without looking. All or nothing. What's the worst that can happen? Well, this has to be pretty fucking high on the list.

Magic existed. And it thought she was as much of a freak as the rest of the world did.

"I don't think I've explained this right," Abigail said quickly.

Meaghan swayed. "No, I think I've got it, thanks," she muttered. "I should leave before he wakes up."

"I'm sure that's not—Jasper! Come in here and—"

"Caine said he wants to destroy the shifter part of himself. Which you're saying is the part of him that wants anything to do with me." Meaghan stared at her hand, clamped like a limpet onto Caine's. Her knuckles were showing white through her skin.

She took a deep breath. *Let go. Let go.* Her arm shook.

"Abigail? What's wrong?" Jasper burst through the door.

Meaghan let go of Caine's hand.

Ruby started to scream.

Abigail cupped the baby's head and turned to her husband. "What's happening?"

Meaghan hovered, still at Caine's side. Her stomach twisted. Ruby's screams were like knives in her ears. Jasper was staggering, his face white, and Caine—

Meaghan's world spun down until all she could hear was her own breathing. Caine was pale as death and completely still. She hadn't noticed that she could see his chest moving with each breath until it stopped.

Opal rushed past her and checked Caine's pulse. His head fell to one side.

All the sound flooded back into the universe.

"—call the doctor. *Now*, I don't care if she isn't a shifter. We'll work something out. Abigail, you know CPR, don't you?"

Abigail nodded. "Jasper, take Ruby, I'll—"

"What's happening?" Meaghan whispered. Her hand felt cold. Her whole body felt cold. She closed her eyes and saw a roaring empty darkness with no end.

She opened her eyes, gasping. "Wake up!" she yelled, so loudly the windows rattled. "Damn it, Caine, *wake up!* Don't you *dare* die! Wake up right now!"

CHAPTER FIFTEEN

Caine

Everything was dark. And cold. Caine was falling—and his creature was falling too, he realized now, not dragging him down but tumbling into the darkness, as helpless as he was, following a tiny fleck of golden light that was disappearing into the shadows below them.

He hadn't realized how weak the monster was. It had always seemed so strong and wild. But he'd told it Meaghan despised what it was, what *he* was, and now it was dying. Just like he'd dreamed of for so long.

And he was falling too. Dying, too.

"Wake up!"

Meaghan's voice blazed through the darkness. Caine gasped. Far away, he felt his heart start to beat again.

"Wake up right now!"

Her command wrapped around him like a lasso. The sheer force of her will, her longing, pulled him up out of the darkness.

Her name was on his lips the moment he was back in his body. He tried once, twice, convincing his tongue to form the word.

"Meaghan?"

"Caine! Don't you *dare* scare me like that!"

He opened his eyes. Meaghan's face was inches from his, blurry and unfocused. He blinked. Her eyes were still blurry. A hot tear fell onto his cheek and she wiped her face hurriedly.

"What happened?" Caine asked. He remembered... darkness. And the tiniest fleck of light, preceding them into the dark and cold.

He rubbed his chest and searched inside himself. His demon was still there, wrapped in a tight unhappy ball in the shadows of his soul. The weakest glimmer of light flickered from between its claws.

"You were—I thought you were—" Meaghan wiped her eyes again and paused with her hands over her face. "But you're... you're fine. And I need to go. I need to go, *now*."

"Wait!" Caine pushed himself up on his elbows. His head spun. The room was crowded. Jasper and Abigail and their baby, Opal and Hank, even Cole standing wide-eyed in the doorway.

"Did you *die*?" Cole's eyes were like dinner plates. "Mom, did he die? My dragon says he died."

"He's fine now, kiddo." Opal's voice was reassuring, but the skin around her eyes was tight. Caine glanced at her, and then back to Meaghan.

"Did you all feel it?" Abigail sounded faint. "Ruby did. I think I got an... echo." Her voice firmed up. "I think I'll sit down."

Caine sat up to make space on the sofa. Jasper was at Abigail's side at once, helping her sit down. His dragon was an almost physical presence, wrapping its care and attention around Abigail and Ruby.

Someone touched his shoulder. Not Meaghan. She was still standing a few feet away, hands clasped white-knuckled in front of her.

135

"How do you feel?" Opal asked.

Caine considered. He didn't take his eyes off Meaghan. "It's still there," he said at last. "The monster."

Meaghan closed her eyes and looked down. "All right," she whispered, so quietly that he wouldn't have heard it if the demon hadn't lent him its sensitive hearing. She unclasped her hands and clenched them into fists at her sides.

"Why do you call it a monster?" Opal's question needled into his brain.

"Because that's what it is." He was answering for Meaghan's sake. She needed to know why he had to stay away from her. "A monster. A hellhound. Something no other shifter I've met had seen, but they all knew to be afraid of it. Including you."

He checked on the creature again. Its eyes were burning marbles, its lips stretched back over sharp fangs. But it didn't move.

"It's a hunter. It terrifies people, and when they're scared enough, it chases them. Hunts them down." He looked up at Meaghan, bracing himself for her horror and fear. "I don't let it. I haven't let it out since the new year and I won't. Not ever again. I won't let it hurt anyone."

Meaghan tipped her head back. Her mouth was tight, but he couldn't read the expression on her face. Not horror. Not fear. But...

"That's twelve months." Opal. And *she* sounded horrified. "Don't you know how dangerous that is? Didn't your parents tell you?"

"My parents aren't shifters. None of my family is." He laughed hollowly. "They'd have me locked up if I told them I thought I had some sort of monstrous creature in my soul. I wasn't born like this, it was done to me. Last Christmas."

"But—"

Hank put a hand on his wife's shoulder. "Opal. The poor guy just came back from the dead. You're going to hound him back there with your questions."

Opal put her hand over his and leaned against him. "Always the sensible one," she murmured, and kissed his hand.

Caine's heart twisted. Inside him, the creature whined, stretching its neck out towards Meaghan.

"There's nothing about it that you don't hate?" Meaghan's eyes were guarded.

Caine straightened. "I need to get rid of it. It's the only way I can be myself again." He ran one hand over his jaw and stared up at Meaghan again. "This isn't *me*. Maybe the man I used to be is gone forever. I can't go back to who I was. But if I can get rid of this monster, I can be someone worth being again."

And someone worth being with. Someone who can give you the love and protection you deserve.

The corners of Meaghan's mouth tightened. Her head jerked back. "Okay. Understood."

Caine stood up. He hadn't meant to; but Meaghan's breath had stuttered halfway through that last word and his legs moved before he even thought about it. "Meaghan—"

"I said I get it, okay? We don't need to, to get into it in front of everyone." She rubbed her hands over the tops of her thighs. "I should go. I have work. Hank, could you look at my truck? It wasn't working last night."

"Sure," Hank said. He exchanged a look with Opal and pain throbbed against Caine's skull. Hank nodded. "Ah, Meaghan. Nasty day out there, if you want to wait in—"

"I'll come with you," she declared. "If I knew more about how that hunk of junk works then none of this would have happened."

That stung. Caine watched her go, head held high, spine so

137

stiff he was worried it might snap.

The front door slammed with a sense of finality.

Caine's head throbbed. "Do you mind?" he said, his voice harsher than he'd intended. "You talking like that gives me a headache."

"And I can't even tell when you *are* telepathing," Abigail added. She slowly smoothed her shirt beneath the baby-carrier, and smiled mirthlessly at Ruby. "Well. What a mess, eh, bubs? Whoever called Christmas the most wonderful time of the year never visited Pine Valley."

Jasper made a face. "It's not that bad—"

"Oh, believe me, darling, it definitely is." Abigail stood up and pointed at Caine. "That woman is his *mate*, and he just told her that he wants to get rid of the part of himself that loves her."

Everyone stared at Caine. He stared back.

"What's a mate?"

The roar of Meaghan's truck broke through the misty morning silence. Inside him, Caine's hellhound howled.

CHAPTER SIXTEEN

Meaghan

Merry fucking Christmas Eve-Eve-Eve-Eve to me. The sign out the front of Puppy Express was like a slap in the face. This Christmas wasn't even going to be regular bad, it was going to *suck ass.*

And the sign was out of date. Meaghan stripped off the fifth "Eve", scraped the snow off her boots and kicked the front door with all her strength. It slammed open and crashed against the wall.

Six feet away, Olly jumped, sending a display of plushie sled dogs flying. "Meaghan!"

The door bounced back off the wall and clicked shut. Meaghan stared at it without seeing it. She was panting.

Hank had fixed the truck so quickly and easily, Caine was sure to think she'd been lying about it having broken down. He'd think—

She shook her head and kicked the door again. This time it didn't move.

It doesn't matter what he thinks, remember? He doesn't want anything to do with you. He's probably over the freaking moon that you left so quickly. One more part of his shifter life he wants to get rid of.

Just file this one under monumental fuckups and move on with your life. Like maybe to Canada this time. It's not like anyone here will want anything to do with you now.

The door opened just as she was aiming another kick at it.

"Meaghan?" Olly's pale hazel eyes were wide. "What happened? Are you okay?"

Meaghan's heart hammered in her chest. She could feel tears at the edge of each breath, waiting to take over. A part of her she thought she'd left behind years before wanted to collapse into tears and have someone, *anyone*, look after her.

But that wasn't going to happen. It *never* happened.

"I'm fine," she choked out.

"I'm sorry, I don't think you are?" Olly looked flustered, which was so un-Olly-like that Meaghan felt the ground swoop under her feet again. Her eyes flew to Olly's face. Specifically, to her red, puffy eyes.

Meaghan's ribs felt tight.

"What happened? Did they come back?"

"What?" Olly blinked at her.

Meaghan breathed in with difficulty. Her ribs were so tight it hurt. "Olly, you look almost as freaked out as you did yesterday. Did the hellhounds come back and do something else?"

Olly touched the puffy skin under her eyes. "Oh, no, I just… didn't sleep well…" She was obviously tiptoeing around the truth.

You and Jackson? Meaghan choked on the words. Right now, she didn't want to hear about anyone else's happy new relationships.

Olly turned her head from side to side, as though she was inspecting Meaghan carefully with each eye.

"If I'm looking freaked out, it's probably because you just kicked your way in here looking as though you're about to burst out crying," she said slowly.

140

And no one wants to see headstrong, bull-in-a-china-shop Meaghan sobbing. What a horrifying thought.

Meaghan plastered on a grin. "I'm fine. Really. Is Bob in?"

"He's out checking the tracks. Meaghan—"

"But he brought the sleigh in from the woods, didn't he? I'll go check it. Make sure it's ready for the parade." *There has to be something I can do right, even if it's just tying tinsel to a dogsled.*

She edged past Olly, into the building. The twinkling lights and decorations hurt her eyes, and the heat from the cheerful log fire was stifling.

Good thing I'm heading outside, then. This is fine. Everything's going to be fine.

"But what *happened*? Did Caine—"

The fragile grip Meaghan had on the emotion boiling inside her slipped. "I don't want to talk about what happened with Caine!"

She pushed out through the back door to the kennels before she could say anything else and gasped as an icy blast hit her face.

Without meaning to, she turned to face the valley where Caine was staying. The low clouds hid that part of the mountains completely. There was no trace of the valley, or the cottage...

...Or any dragons, or ghost gang, or Caine. Or his... hellhound. She gulped down another lungful of air so cold it burned.

Burning. Like Caine's eyes the first time she looked at him. Like that strange feeling of joy that had radiated out of them.

Had that been his hellhound? But it hadn't felt dangerous. Just joyful.

Another thing she'd gotten wrong.

"Meaghan!" Olly burst through the door after her.

"I'm *busy*!" Meaghan bawled back.

She didn't know why Olly was being so persistent. After

everything she'd put her through since she moved to Pine Valley, and then abandoning her yesterday after the ghost gang had stolen the dogs—the *hellhound shifters*, she corrected herself—she was surprised Olly was even speaking to her at all.

Excited barks followed her as she strode past the kennel yard where the dogs were relaxing. The tight band around her chest relaxed a bit. The dogs usually made her feel better. They were so boundlessly cheerful and easy to please.

She paused to scratch a few ears, but their happy faces just reminded her of Caine, lounging in the dog box with them. Shirtless. Happy.

"Where's that stupid sleigh?" she muttered angrily.

"The one we brought back from the woods? It's in the shed." Jackson was leaning against the shed in question, arms folded. There were purple shadows under his eyes.

Someone else who 'didn't sleep well', Meaghan thought. Her ribs ached. *And who probably can't wait to see the back of me.*

"Thanks," she muttered. She put her head down and headed for the shed door, but not quick enough. Jackson's voice followed her.

"Everything all right, Megs?"

"*Fine,*" she gritted out as she stormed past him.

He peeled himself off the side of the shed. His voice was strangely desperate. "How did last night—"

"I don't want to talk about it!"

Whatever he said next sounded like swearing, but she slammed the shed door too quickly to hear it properly. She leaned against it, panting.

Why are they pretending to care that I'm upset? I'm just going to mess up everyone's day. Like I always do.

I should have gone home. Except it isn't home, it's just a place with all my stuff, and Pine Valley isn't my home anymore, it can't be. And not for the usual reason. Not because they're all normal and I'm a freak. Because they're all magical, and I'm—I'm—

Jackson knocked on the door and called through it, "Hey, Megs, everything all right?"

"I'm *fine!*" she yelled back, pounding her fist into the wood. Something clattered to the concrete floor.

She looked down. The 'Eve' sign she'd been carrying, which was only made of thin plywood, had cracked in two.

Good job ruining it, Meaghan. She squeezed her eyes shut until the hot feeling in them went away.

"Shit," she muttered, and scooped up the broken pieces. She looked around the shed. Half of it was used for storage for the Puppy Express hire sleds—the cutesy two-person ones for couples on romantic snow rides, and the big family-sized ones with seatbelts to stop kids running off into the winter wonderland. The far end was set up as a workshop, and Meaghan stomped towards it.

The Santa sleigh that the hellhound shifters had stolen was sitting in the middle of the workspace. Now that it was out of the snow, Meaghan could see how much damage the joyride had done. The old-fashioned wooden runners were scraped and pitted, and there were long scratches in the red and green paint on the body. Almost all the tinsel and fake holly had been torn off and the only bell left tied to it looked like it had been smashed flat with a hammer.

She gently placed the broken sign on the workbench and sighed. *At least fixing that all up is going to keep you busy*, she told herself.

Something moved in the corner of her eye. Meaghan looked up just in time to see a shadow flit away from one of the shed's windows.

She narrowed her eyes. *Olly?*

Behind her, the door creaked. "Meaghan?"

Meaghan blinked. That wasn't the voice she'd been expecting. It was Jackson.

Jackson, calling her *Meaghan*, not *Megs*.

Her stomach went cold. Something must be *really* wrong, if Jackson was using her full name.

"Hey, Meaghan," Jackson said awkwardly, standing with his hands in his pockets. "Are you... is everything okay?"

She spun around to face him. "Why does everyone keep asking me that?"

"Oh, I dunno. Probably because you look like you're about to fall down crying, and none of us really thought that was possible." Jackson eased his way into the room. "What's up?"

"What's up is I've got three days to fix up this sleigh for the Santa parade and you're distracting me from my work and—and creeping around like I'm some wild animal you're trying not to scare off," Meaghan snapped. "I thought you were a deputy, not a park ranger. Or—or whatever you really are."

"What's that supposed to mean?" Jackson's eyes were suddenly wary, and something inside Meaghan snapped.

"Fine. Fine! You want to know what's wrong? I thought I'd finally found somewhere I actually fit in, and now it turns out all the people I thought were my friends here were *lying* to me the whole time."

Jackson looked like a deer in the headlights. "Ah, shit," he muttered.

Meaghan threw her arms up. "That's all you have to say?"

Wood creaked behind her, and a soft breeze chilled the back of her neck.

Great. Here comes Olly, inspecting the situation from all angles before she makes her presence known.

Jackson stared at her, eyes hard as though he was winding himself up to throw her anger back at her. Then he glanced behind her. His face creased and he looked away.

Meaghan spun around, catching Olly in the middle of walking up to her. *Sneaking* up to her.

"And what do you want?" she demanded.

Olly froze and blinked at her. Meaghan glared at her, then over her shoulder at Jackson again. Neither of them said anything.

"Oh come on," she burst out. "I *know*, okay? I know about shifters. I know that the Heartwells are dragons and that *you*, Jackson, have been keeping me away from investigating the ghost gang because everyone thought they were shifters too. And they are, by the way. Hellhound shifters. So you might as well tell me whatever else there is to know."

Jackson opened his mouth, but Olly got in first.

"It sounds like you know the big stuff already," she burst out. "So there's no point keeping everything else a secret. I'm an owl shifter."

Meaghan stared at her and she waved back, a half-hearted smile on her face.

"Snowy owl shifter. That's why my folks were so keen for me to come and work for Uncle Bob for a while. Let my owl stretch its wings a bit, somewhere it wouldn't be as obvious as the city."

Her eyes flicked past Meaghan to where Jackson was standing, and the barely-a-smile dropped off her face.

"Not that it deserves it," she muttered, folding her arms and ducking her head. "Stupid bird."

Meaghan looked back at Jackson in time to see him hide a pained expression. "What am I missing here?" she demanded. "You might as well tell me. It can't be bigger than freaking *dragons*."

Jackson's lips pressed together. "Nothing," he said, a trace of resignation in his voice. "Unfortunately."

"What do you mean, unfortunately?" Meaghan heard her own voice getting higher and higher. "Is there some other horrible thing I don't know about?"

Jackson drew in a breath that made him wince.

"Ma's a deer shifter. I'm not. She was keen for me to move to Pine Valley for the same reason Olly's parents were. Hoped being around other shifters might make a switch flip inside me, or something. But it didn't. There. Now you know everything."

Meaghan's neck was aching from looking back and forth between Olly and Jackson. She leaned against the workbench so she could see them both at once, and frowned.

Was it her imagination, or without her as a buffer standing between them, were Olly and Jackson even more awkward around each other than usual?

Remember Jackson's text message? They were together last night. And now...

They must be mates. And they're awkward because I'm here, getting in the way.

"Go on," Jackson muttered. "I know you're dying to ask."

Meaghan opened her mouth—then shut it and shook her head. "It's none of my business. None of this is any of my business, is it? I don't belong here and everything I've done has only made things worse."

She stared at the floor. She didn't even feel like crying, now. Just empty and exhausted. *Can't even be sad properly. Figures.*

"Meaghan..."

She could almost *feel* Olly looking at her. Inspecting her, in that careful, consider-all-angles way that she did everything. Tipping her head from side to side. Owlishly. Hah.

146

Any other time, Meaghan might have laughed.

Olly leaned against the workbench beside her and slipped one arm tentatively around her shoulder.

"What happened with Caine?"

"It didn't work out." Meaghan's voice was a tiny, unhappy thread. Her ribs were aching with the pressure of holding herself together and suddenly, she couldn't do it anymore. "Caine thinks he's a monster. Everything was going so well, and then his hellhound popped up and I'm his mate, apparently, and since he hates his hellhound so much that means he doesn't want anything to do with me. The end."

"So he is a shifter. You were right about that, Olly." Jackson said carefully. "And you're his mate."

"Yes. Apparently." Meaghan didn't look at either of them.

"But that's a good thing," Olly objected.

"Except it's me. And if there's one thing I'm good at, it's making good things go bad."

"That's not true!" Olly squeezed her shoulders. "What about yesterday? You found the dogs."

"And left you alone after a group of hellhound shifters scared the h— scared you!"

"I was *fine*," Olly insisted. "Besides, if you'd waited around for Bob to come back, he never would have given the go-ahead for you to go out on your own. Because of the…"

"Hellhound shifters." Jackson's voice was heavy. "That's what you said they were. The same as Caine?" Meaghan nodded and he scrubbed one hand through his hair. "First I couldn't stop you from investigating the mystery shifters, and now you've gone and solved it on your own."

"I wanted to save Christmas, not… discover a secret world of people who can turn into crazy animals," Meaghan replied. "And

I haven't done that. We still don't know where the hellhound shifters are, or what they're going to do next. Or why they're doing all this in the first place."

"But we know what they are. That'll help. *You've* helped."

Meaghan sighed.

Maybe things aren't as bad as I thought. Maybe I haven't ruined everything.

"I just hope you two had a better night than I did," she muttered, and Olly's arm went stiff around her shoulders. Meaghan raised her head, confused, but neither of them met her eyes. "But I thought you two…?"

"It didn't work out," Jackson said shortly. "One more thing that's wrong with me—forget it. I'd better go and keep an eye on the front desk."

He stomped out. Olly watched him go, pained yearning in her eyes. Meaghan's heart twisted in sympathy. She knew that if Caine were here, she'd be looking at him with exactly the same expression.

But what hap—

She didn't let herself finish the thought.

Don't stick your nose in. Don't make it worse. Don't get into other people's business…

But Olly had chased her out here when she saw she was upset. Maybe, just once, she could barge in and help, instead of screwing things up worse.

Meaghan took a deep breath. "You want to talk about it?"

Olly sniff-gulped and sagged against Meaghan's side. "I thought I had it all figured out!"

"You'd inspected the situation from all possible angles?" Meaghan joked weakly, putting an arm around her.

"I liked Jackson from the *moment* I saw him. He got the deputy job a few months before you moved to Pine Valley, and came around to introduce himself to all the local businesses. I thought my snowy owl was interested, too, but…" She gnawed on her lip. "Maybe I waited too long. I don't know if that's even possible. But last night I made a move, and my owl was just like… *No, thank you.*"

"But that's not so bad, is it? I mean… isn't that just a normal relationship? And Jackson's human, so if he likes you and you like him…"

Olly was shaking her head. She sniffed again and said in a small voice, "He knows it's not the real thing. That there's still someone out there that my owl wants more than him. You know Jackson's mom brought him up by herself?"

"Yeah." Meaghan had needled that out of him the first week she was in Pine Valley.

"His dad was a shifter, too, but they weren't mates. He says he doesn't want to make the same mistake his mom made." Olly was crying now, but they were angry tears. "He thinks he's a mistake! Can you believe that? He's not, he's grumpy and reliable and *wonderful* and my owl is an *asshole.*"

Olly wiped her face and hiccupped. "I'm sorry. I came out here to check if you were all right, not…"

Her voice trailed off. Meaghan knew what she was going to say, though. *Not talk about my own troubles.*

Olly was her closest friend in Pine Valley—and not just because she'd been the first person Meaghan met with a spare sofa. Her strange mixture of being chill and carefully scoping out situations before she got into them had meshed perfectly with Meaghan's complete lack of chill and tendency to throw herself into things without looking. Not to mention the fact that she was always filling Meaghan's pockets with useful things like handwarmers.

And there was one thing they always agreed on. The Puppy Express was magical not just because of the amazing snowy tracks and view across the mountains, or the dogsled-delivered Christmas cards. It was because no one could be around sled dogs and be unhappy.

"I know something that might help." Meaghan stood up, pulling Olly with her. "Come on."

There was no sign of Jackson outside. Meaghan kept an eye out for him as she took Olly over to the kennels, but her gaze kept slipping up over the trees to the cloud-covered mountaintops and the hidden snowy valley where Caine was staying.

Her chest felt like it was about to burst.

The Heartwells are with him, she reminded herself. *They're shifters, like him. They'll know how to help him.*

Won't they?

CHAPTER SEVENTEEN

Caine

Opal put her hands on Caine's shoulders and pushed him down into the kitchen chair. He sat down, too tired and miserable to object. The Heartwells had given him some time to recover after Meaghan left, but now they were all gathered around. Even baby Ruby looked serious.

"Right," Opal said, crossing her arms. "Tell me everything you know about shifters."

"I know *lots* about shifters!" Cole piped up from behind her. She sighed and reached out without looking to ruffle his hair.

"Yes, kiddo, but I'm asking Mr. Guinness."

"I could help him!"

"I think you've helped enough today, champ," Hank rumbled. Cole's face fell.

Caine roused himself enough to defend the tiny dragon shifter. "Don't blame him for what happened this morning. It's all my fault. And it would have been worse if he wasn't here."

Hank dragged over another chair and Opal sat down in it, arms still crossed.

"What do you mean, it would have been worse?" she asked.

Caine's gut twisted. His hellhound was hunkered down inside him, so thickly wreathed in black smoke that the only trace of it was the slight glow of its eyes.

"Because if I'd been the only shifter she ever met, she might not have seen how wrong I am. Now she's gone, and that's…" Caine dropped his head into his hands. "That's the best outcome I could have hoped for."

The room was silent. Even Cole didn't say anything.

Opal cleared her throat. "You said you don't know what a mate is?" she said slowly.

"No. But my hellhound thinks Meaghan is one, so it can't be good." Caine groaned. "She's the best goddamned thing that's ever happened to me. I can't let her get caught up in this nightmare."

"If she's your mate then she *is* the best thing that's ever happened to you. Trust me." Jasper wrapped an arm around Abigail's shoulders and pulled her close to him.

"And good luck *letting* her do anything," Abigail added, jiggling Ruby. "Meaghan's only been here six months and she's already a legend. Nothing stands in her way. Not even poor Jackson after you lot saddled him with keeping her away from the ghost gang problem."

"Which she's solved." Jasper reached a finger out for Ruby to grab. "I don't know about the rest of you, but having just spent the last two months flying my wings to stubs trying to track down the shifters who've been causing trouble, I'm feeling slightly embarrassed that Meaghan figured it all out despite our best efforts to solve it ourselves *and* keep her away."

"It's almost as though keeping humans in the dark is a bad thing," Abigail teased. "Where have we learned that before, I wonder?"

Her teasing grin softened as Jasper caught her chin and kissed her on the forehead. Caine's chest ached. Movement stirred inside him.

Burning eyes blazed through the smoke. His hellhound's anger sent lightning down his spine.

He must have made some sort of noise, because the next moment, all eyes were on him.

"You *knew*?" he gasped out. Smoke blurred the edges of his vision. "You knew something was attacking the town, and you kept her in the dark? She could have been hurt!"

When he'd thought Meaghan's presence had exorcised his hellhound from him, the idea of her chasing wrong-doers by herself had made him admire her. Now it terrified him.

"Mr. Guinness, we—"

"What if it had been the other hellhounds she found in the forest yesterday, not me?"

Caine had stood up so quickly that his chair clattered over behind him. Jasper was in front of him at once, his hands on Caine's shoulders.

"Then we wouldn't be having this conversation, because I'm guessing by the way you just reacted that your hellhound would have smashed the mountain to pieces to save her. And then you'd have to admit your hellhound isn't any danger to her."

Caine grabbed Jasper's wrists and glared into his eyes, but the dragon shifter didn't back down.

"You don't think my hellhound's dangerous?" he growled. "I saw you flinch when it saw you outside. All of you. Or have you forgotten already?"

A shiver went down his spine. *This is it. I've lost everything. My job. My old life. Meaghan. What more do I have to lose?*

"Abigail, you'd better take the baby and Cole and get out of here," he said, his voice gravely with exhaustion. "I'm going to show the dragons what happens when I let go of my hellhound's leash."

Jasper stepped in front of his wife and child. Caine's heart twisted. *He's protecting them. Like I have to protect Meaghan, by staying away from her.*

His hellhound was straining to be free. All he had to do was let go of its chains. It jumped up, muscles bunching with months of repressed energy, fire blazing from its eyes.

Caine braced himself as it rose closer to the surface. His senses. Thick hairs sprouted on his arms. His teeth lengthened. His eyes burned.

As terrified as he was at the thought of his hellhound being free, he was relieved, as well. Once the dragon shifters saw what he really was, they would lock him up, and he wouldn't be able to hurt anyone else.

Sparks flared and burst in the smoke edging his vision as he stared at each of the gathered Heartwells. The monster was behind his eyes, *in* his eyes, looking out at them all.

But this time, none of them flinched.

And he didn't transform. The monster retreated, its frustration a blackboard-scratch down Caine's spine.

They aren't the ones we're looking for, it muttered, its voice the crackle of splintering wood. *They're not the ones our mate is hunting!*

Caine clutched his forehead. The demon's voice hurt as much as the other shifters' telepathy did.

But there was something else, as well. When the hellhound said *our mate*, something like a matchstick flared inside Caine, in the center of his soul where he chained his hellhound away. A soft, golden light.

His hellhound wrapped itself around the light. *Our mate*, it growled softly. *Ours.*

Strong hands led him back to the kitchen table. He sat with his head in his hands.

"It won't let her go," he whispered. "Will it?"

"No." Opal's voice was gentle, but firm.

"Then I need to do what I came here to do." Caine raised his head and met her eyes. "I need you to help me destroy it."

CHAPTER EIGHTEEN

Meaghan

"*Ouch.*" Meaghan clutched her chest and swayed.

"Are you all right?" Olly looked up at her from the pile of puppies. She still had her arms stretched over as many of them as she could reach, like a broody chicken on a nest of strange, barking eggs.

Or like an owl on… whatever owls did.

"I'm…" *fine.* The word was on the tip of her tongue. Meaghan frowned and rubbed her chest again. "Just a cramp, I think."

"Is it your neck again?"

Meaghan stared at Olly in surprise. "I never told you there was anything wrong with my neck."

Somehow, without moving at all or breaking eye contact, Olly managed to convey a whole-body eye-roll. "Meaghan, I have a tiny, asshole predator living inside my brain. It noticed you rubbing your neck about twenty seconds after we first met. Why do you think I kept slipping you instant handwarmers?"

Meaghan realized she was still rubbing her neck subconsciously. She snapped her hand down again. "So that my hands didn't freeze when I was out with the dogs?"

"No, because heat is good for sore muscles! I know humans don't heal up as well as shifters do, so I researched this *very* thoroughly! I always—" Olly's face fell. "But maybe I'm wrong. Like with Jackson. I thought that I had that all sorted out, too."

"You're right. Heat does help. I guess my neck's been bad for so long, I forget about it unless it's really bad."

"Like now?" Olly's pale hazel eyes blinked at her and Meaghan dropped her hand again.

Her face felt hot and cold at the same time. There was no way she was going to explain to Olly that she'd been touching her neck because she was remembering how wonderful it felt when Caine massaged all the knots out of it.

All the knots were back now, of course. And the happy memory was all twisted up with the misery of Caine rejecting her. *Hating* her.

"Why?" she said out loud, and shook her head when she saw Olly's face crease. "I mean, why did you care?"

"Because I like you," Olly replied. "I'm not good at making friends, and I know you'd already decided I was your friend when you moved all your stuff into my living room, but I wanted to be friends back at you."

Meaghan knelt beside her and scruffled Loony's ears. "So you said it with handwarmers?"

"It's better than saying it with a freshly killed mouse." Olly smiled shyly.

"God, was that the other option? Handwarmers, please." Meaghan laughed as Parkour scooched past Loony to wriggle onto her lap. She gave up on kneeling and sat down, letting the dogs climb over her like wriggly, wet-nosed blankets.

Like when they'd all cuddled up with Caine in the back of her truck.

Meaghan's stomach lurched. *Can't be unhappy around sled dogs, huh? When will you learn how wrong you are about everything?*

She hugged Parkour tighter, trying desperately to ignore the ache in her chest.

"For the record, someone moving into your house without even asking if you're okay with them staying isn't the sort of thing a friend does. It's the sort of thing a weird, pushy person with no boundaries does."

"Hmm. Sounds like you all right." Olly lay back. She didn't look happy, not exactly, but the tense wariness was easing from her face.

"Just don't let anyone else do it."

Olly peered at her over the sea of dogs. "I'm not a total push-over, Meaghan. I wouldn't have let you take over my living room if I didn't want you there."

"Oh." Meaghan had never even considered that. She always pushed herself in, and eventually people got annoyed enough that they pushed her out again.

They never actually wanted her to be there.

"Why are you saying all this, anyway?" Olly asked, her eyes narrowing. "This sounds suspiciously like the advice my parents loaded me down with before they packed me off up here."

Meaghan rested her chin on Parkour's head. She didn't look at Olly, but she didn't need to; she could practically feel the younger woman's eyes boring into her.

"Caine thinks he's a monster."

She realized, too late, that she wasn't just staring into space; she was looking out towards the valley she'd already started thinking of as *Caine's valley.* She blinked and focused on Parkour's ears.

"But we both know that's not true, right?"

Meaghan blinked. "What?"

"You said he's a hellhound shifter, and so are the guys who stole the dogs yesterday. *They* were monsters. When they looked at me it was like they could see straight into my worst memories. All the things I felt guilty about. Like not telling Jackson how I felt." Olly grimaced. "And we both know how well *that* went. But Caine's different."

"How can you tell?"

"Because of how he was looking at you. I couldn't tell what sort of shifter he was yesterday, but I knew he had to be *something*. There was just a hint of something different about him. Plus he had that dopey, smitten look. Like he'd do anything you asked."

Meaghan laughed despite herself. "When I first saw him, I told him not to run away, and it was like his feet were glued to the ground."

"There! See?"

Just for a moment, hope flared in Meaghan's heart. Then she shook herself. "But it doesn't matter, does it? Either he manages to get rid of his hellhound and he has no reason to want anything to do with me anymore, or he doesn't, and I'm just an add-on to something he hates."

Olly reached out and nudged Meaghan's leg with her foot. "Come on. There's a third option. Out with it."

Meaghan stared at her and she rolled her eyes.

"You *must* be thinking it! Come on. You say he thinks he's a monster. But what do you think? You must have seen his hellhound, if it decided you're his mate."

"I…" *Burning eyes. Bright, heart-leaping joy.* "I think so."

"And was it a monster? Did it make you feel like your brain was being melted away with acid until the only thing left was all the things you hated about yourself?"

"No!" *I don't need a hellhound shifter for that.*

"Well, then, what are you waiting for?" Olly laughed. "I don't know why I'm asking. You're *you*. Of course you're going to go and get him."

Go and get him?

"Olly, I—"

Meaghan buried her face in Parkour's fur to stop herself talking. Her head was reeling.

Olly had so much trust in her. She acted like there was no question that Meaghan would storm back up the mountain and demand Caine take her back.

Because that was the Meaghan she knew. Headstrong. Take-no-shit-from-anybody. Pushing herself in where she wasn't wanted. Running at life like it was a road full of potholes, thinking that at least if she went down hard she'd bounce out again.

It had gotten her this far in life. But it always came crashing down in the end. And it was too late to wish that when everything did come crashing down at last, it would hurt less.

Wasn't she ever going to learn?

Face still buried in Parkour's warm fur, Meaghan rubbed her chest. The wrenching pain that had struck before had faded, but a ghost of it was still there, like a pulled muscle that still hurt.

She'd never thought having a broken heart would be so literal. But…

Olly couldn't be right, could she?

She thought back to that first moment she'd set eyes on Caine. To the smoky fire in his eyes that she'd told herself she was imagining. And the sheer joy that had poured out of them.

If that was his hellhound, his so-called "monster", then maybe he *was* wrong about it. Maybe it wasn't a monster at all, just something new and strange that he didn't entirely understand.

Hope sparked in Meaghan's chest, a brief, fluttering burst of light in the exact place that had hurt only a few moments ago.

And if Caine's hellhound wasn't a monster then maybe he—

Meaghan shook her head. *Stop fooling yourself. Olly hasn't even seen Caine's hellhound. Jasper and the other Heartwells have, and you saw how they reacted.*

Whatever they saw in him, it scared *them. And if it didn't scare you...*

Her neck and shoulder muscles clenched. Pain shot down from the knot in her neck, straight to her chest, and the tiny golden spark of hope vanished.

When will you learn how wrong you are about everything?

If it didn't scare you, then there must be something wrong with you.

CHAPTER NINETEEN

Caine

DECEMBER 23
(CHRISTMAS EVE EVE)

Meaghan's skin was soft under Caine's hands. He ran the backs of his fingers along her waist, and her delighted shiver of laughter filled him with a joy deeper than anything he'd ever felt. He leaned over her, lowered his face towards hers, and frowned.

"Why are we back in the city?" He looked around. They weren't lying on his bed; they were on pavement. Asphalt grated against Caine's knees. Graffiti covered the alley walls.

I know this place.

He looked down. Meaghan was gone. He was alone. Not even his hellhound was with him.

Ice ran down his spine.

Not this nightmare again.

He tried to stand up, but his legs wouldn't obey. His lungs cramped.

This is just a dream. I can make it stop. Just wake up, wake up,

WAKE UP—

Silence poured from the end of the alleyway. Fiery eyes burned, turning even the puddles of light from the streetlights into pitchy shadows.

It's a dream. I can control this. I'm not in the alleyway. I'm asleep in my bed. In my home.

He turned a corner and stopped. The alleyway was gone. Early morning sun filtered through narrow blinds, catching motes of dust in the air. He was in his old office, where he'd worked so many long hours.

Caine sat down at his desk.

What was I working on?

A property scam. That was it. Something Angus had asked him to look into. *Let's see if you can crack this*, he'd said.

All the information was here. Everything they needed to take the scam down. Caine opened the manila file, sorting through newspaper articles and his own notes and photos.

Well, he'd cracked it. Last night. The last missing link had slotted into place and he'd been on his way home, before...

Dread pooled in his gut. Caine looked down. Blood was pouring from his leg, spilling over the chair, onto the dusty office floor.

"Caine? What the shit are you doing here?"

Caine looked up. Angus was standing in the door, his face slack with shock.

The room spun around Caine. It was all coming back to him. The terrifying, demonic creatures. The chase. The bite on his leg...

He stood up slowly.

And something woke up inside him.

"No!"

Caine woke up gasping. He sat up on the edge of the bed, head in his hands, stomach churning.

163

The nightmare had never gone on that long before. It had always stopped in the alley.

He stumbled to the bathroom and splashed his face with cold water. The face that stared back at him from the mirror was wan and drawn.

Caine's hellhound whined, and he flinched.

It must be a warning from my subconscious, he decided. He started drying his face and had to stop and brace himself against the vanity as a wave of faintness rolled over him. *A reminder not to forget what my hellhound is capable of.*

He didn't remember much of what had happened after his hellhound woke up that first time. Just flashes.

He'd transformed. It had hurt. And the shock in Angus' eyes had turned to fear, and he'd chased his oldest friend like a demon out of hell, until…

Caine shook his head. His memories were all muddled up. The hellhounds chasing him. Him chasing Angus. Fighting the hellhounds again, being chased again, chasing him again… The flashes of memory ran together and over each other in his head until he wasn't sure he could trust his own mind.

Whatever had happened that morning, Angus had made it out alive. That was the important thing.

And now Caine knew what he had to do. Opal hadn't wanted to tell him, but apparently there were stories of shifters who'd starved their animals out. Kept them locked inside, not letting them take form… and eventually the creatures just faded away.

It's been a year since I transformed into the monster. It's fought me since then, seen out of my eyes—but never taken form.

I just need to keep it that way, until…

"Guinness? You awake?"

Caine grimaced. The Heartwell men were taking it in shifts

164

to watch over him. Opal's orders. Whoever was down there now would probably spend the day trying to convince him to keep his hellhound.

The nightmare had reminded him why that was a bad idea.

"Guinness? Caine?"

"I'm up!" he called, and gave the mirror one last glance. There was no smoke or fire in his reflection. Just exhaustion.

Good, he thought, and trudged downstairs.

*

Hank Heartwell was that morning's babysitter. He mildly bullied Caine into eating more than just coffee for breakfast, and then broke the news.

"Come on. We're helping out at the Puppy Express today."

"No." Caine set down his fork. "That's Meaghan's workplace. I told you, I can't see her."

"Then don't. Bob needs someone to clear a fallen tree from across the Sweethearts Lake track. They've got a big corporate booking for Christmas Day. Last-minute thing. And who knows, maybe some of them will be after a bit of a holiday romance."

Caine looked at his plate without seeing it. "That's good for the town." *Good for Meaghan.*

"Corporate credit cards? Could be, yeah." Hank stood up, looked at Caine, who wasn't moving, and sighed. "Meaghan and Olly are in town today, checking the route for the parade. We're not going to bump into them."

Caine stood up and grabbed his coat.

The drive to Puppy Express seemed shorter, or maybe it was just that Hank's SUV had better suspension than Meaghan's old truck. Bob waved Hank and Caine in with hardly a glance, and

Caine started to think that maybe this was a good idea, after all.

Having something to do will be better than sitting around with nothing but my own thoughts all day.

That lasted about an hour, until Hank's careful lack of mentioning anything to do with shifters, or Meaghan, or the ghost gang started to get on Caine's nerves.

"So what's the plan?" he said as Hank pointed out the fallen pine lying across the track ahead. "To stop the ghost gang."

"Stop them? Not sure how we're meant to do that."

"But you have to. They won't just leave." Caine panted as he followed Hank to the tree. "Whatever has brought them here, whatever's behind these attacks, they haven't got any reason to stop. Even if it's just pure sadism. Pine Valley is an easy target. Like fish in a barrel."

"Even more so, if we get a big dump of snow and the roads get cut off." Hank whistled softly. "But... Stop an enemy we can't see, or scent, or feel any psychic trace of. That's a hell of a task, and we've failed at it so far."

"But now you know what you're hunting."

"Sure. As soon as you said you thought the gang were hellhounds, the girls started digging into some research. It all matches up. Glowing fiery eyes, impossible for even other shifters to trace. That must be what we've been dealing with the last few months." He sighed. "Or failing to deal with."

Caine's spine tingled. His hellhound pricked up its ears. *The girls? Does he mean Meaghan? Why would she be looking into hellhounds?*

To find a way to protect Pine Valley. That must be it. She's made it clear she doesn't want anything to do with you.

But... Frustration crackled under his skin. "You can't just sit and wait for them to attack again."

"You want to tell us what else we can do?" Hank knelt by the tree. "You take the other side. We'll try to pivot it off the track."

Caine's mind was whirring. The nightmare had done more than remind him of his hellhound's nature; it had reminded him of who he used to be. Someone who solved other people's problems.

What had he told Meaghan? *I'm just a man who wants to help out where I can.* Maybe it was true after all.

He straightened his shoulders. "This is a small town. Tourist numbers are down. Olly knows what the hellhound shifters look like in human form."

Hank nodded. "Jackson's gone door-to-door all the hotels and rentals. No one matches Olly's descriptions."

"They have a base out of town, then. If they're shifters, they're hardy. They might be in a hunting shack, or even camping."

"We can't sense any of them from the air, and that's a hell of a lot of square footage to cover by foot. Lift!"

Caine channeled his frustration into his muscles. He and Hank hoisted the tree easily between them and moved it off the track.

Hank dusted off his hands. "Bit of strength left in you yet, eh?"

Caine opened his mouth, and closed it. "Unfortunately," he muttered.

"Look. Knowing who we're up against is one thing. But we're no better off than we were before. You're right. We're sitting ducks." Hank blew out his cheeks. "Well. Those of us who can fly away in a crisis are sitting ducks. The rest of the town are, as you said, fish in a barrel."

Including Meaghan.

"We could use a hellhound on our side."

"You don't know what you're asking." *But if Meaghan's in danger—*

"Hey! Caine!" Jackson's voice echoed through the woods.

Hank groaned. "Damn it, Jackson, you're meant to be on lookout today."

"Looking out for something even you shifters can't see? Yeah, I'll get right on it." He jerked his chin at Caine. "Right after I've had a chat with our friend here."

Hank stared at him, then glanced at Caine and shrugged. "Kids," he grumbled, even though he had five years at most on Caine. "I'll start heading back. Let Bob know the track's clear."

Caine waited for him to disappear around a turn in the track.

He almost got me. The big dragon shifter was so bluff and hearty, Caine hadn't expected that sort of trickery. Hank had almost managed to get Caine to talk himself into thinking his hellhound might be useful to keep around.

He turned to face Jackson. The younger man had his hands thrust deep in his jacket pockets. His stance was bullish.

"You here to throw a punch?"

"Against a shifter who can walk through walls?" Jackson threw back. Caine tensed, and Jackson cursed. "You wouldn't do it, would you? Use your hellhound powers to avoid a punch. You're that twisted up about it. *Shit.*"

Jackson stalked down the track another few paces and kicked a snow-covered rock.

"The others think you'll get over it. That you're freaking out over being a baby shifter and getting to know your hellhound, and they can jolly you along until you get over yourself and apologize to Meaghan for being an asshole. But you're not, are you? And now she's—*fuck.*"

Caine didn't answer. Jackson swore and kicked the rock again.

"Do you even know how lucky you are?"

"Lucky? I've got a *monster* inside me!"

"You've got a *mate!*" Jackson roared back. "And you're going to let her go, you're going to lose the best thing that can happen to any shifter—any *person*—just because you don't like your hellhound?"

Caine clenched his fists, ready to turn this into a real shouting match, when something in Jackson's expression made him pause.

"You're right. She is the best thing that's ever happened to me. That's why I need to stay away from her."

"You're going to lose her." The steam had gone out of Jackson, as well. "Olly—" He winced. "Olly thinks Meaghan's going to come roaring up here to tell you to pull your head out of your ass, but she doesn't know what it's like. Having that soulmate bond hanging there like a promise, just out of reach, and it being yanked away." He swallowed hard. "Meaghan deserves better than that."

Caine's chest twisted, deep in that spot where his hellhound lay wrapped around a dying candleflame. He rubbed his breastbone, not meeting Jackson's eyes. "No. She deserves better than being the other half of a monster's soul."

"You don't know what you're saying."

"You don't know what I'm dealing with. None of you do," Caine spat out.

"But I know what she's dealing with. And you're running out of time."

"That's the idea." Caine laughed bitterly. "Opal said I can starve the hellhound out. It shouldn't be long now—"

"And you think Meaghan's just going to sit around waiting for you to half-kill yourself?"

Caine froze.

Jackson swore and sat down on the rock he'd been kicking. "I can't turn into some sort of amazing creature, or fly, or read minds

169

or any of that shit, so I've been sitting on my ass doing the only thing that's left. Checking records. Accommodation, rentals—and bus tickets." He shot Caine a hard look. "Meaghan's planning to leave the day after Christmas. She hasn't told anyone."

"She wouldn't just run away without saying anything." Unease stirred in Caine's bones. Slinking off without a fight wasn't like Meaghan. He might not have known her long, but he knew that much.

"Why not? It's what I'm doing. When the deepest part of someone's soul tells you to fuck off, what other choice do you have?" He grimaced. "Or when that part of a person's soul wants you to stay, but the person is trying to get rid of it, and you too. Fuck it. I don't know why I even came out here. But you have a *chance*, and…" His voice trailed off. "That's more than most of us get."

Jackson didn't know why he hated his hellhound, Caine realized. He'd told the Heartwells about Angus, but not anyone else.

Not Meaghan.

"Just talk to her?" Jackson's voice was pleading.

Caine swallowed. "I'll think about it."

Jackson groaned and stood up. "Like Meaghan told Olly she'd think about throwing you into the back of her truck again. You two really are a match."

"If I get rid of my hellhound—"

Jackson waved a hand tiredly. "Sure. Keep telling yourself that." He looked out over the frozen lake at the end of the track that Caine and Hank had cleared. "Meaghan thought the ghost gang was trying to ruin Christmas. God knows why they're really here, but if that was their goal, then they've managed it."

He trod off back through the trees, shoulders hunched.

Caine glanced back along the track. He knew he should go

after Hank, see if there was anything else needed doing—but not yet.

He'd thought the last thing he needed was time alone. But maybe that was wrong.

Caine sighed and trudged over to the lakeside. He could see exactly why Bob had wanted this part of the track cleared. Sweetheart Lake was beautiful. This must be one of the most popular stops in the short dogsled rides that Puppy Express ran for visitors.

There was a small picnic table with a view across the frozen lake that was the perfect spot for a group of friends to stop and chat, or kids to have a snowball fight to let off some energy, or a couple to—

His hellhound shivered and Caine's jaw tensed. *For a couple to do the sort of things Meaghan and I might be doing, if I hadn't…*

His shoulders slumped. *If I didn't have a hellhound lodged inside my soul. If I was the man I used to be.*

…If I hadn't driven her off.

Caine sat down at the picnic table and ran his fingers through his hair.

What am I supposed to do?

The forest was completely silent. He held his head in his hands and stared out across the lake.

Jackson had cut straight to the heart of it. Caine had been holding onto the hope that once he was free of his hellhound, he could go and beg Meaghan's forgiveness.

But why would she want anything to do with him, after the way he'd treated her? He'd as good as told her in front of everyone that he'd rather kill part of himself than be with her.

His hellhound whined and curled itself into a tighter ball. It hid its face under its massive front paws, obscuring its burning eyes and the smoke coiling out of its jaws.

He prodded it warily, expecting it to snap at him, but it didn't. It wasn't angry, or grinding its teeth, or laying low while it planned anything.

It *hurt*.

He prodded it again. In all the time he'd known it, his hellhound had never been like this. Furious, or suspicious, or exultant with its evil glee at chasing people, but never this gray, listless hurt.

It was almost enough to make him feel sorry for it.

What about you? Don't you want to go to her?

If it jumped at the thought, if it started talking about hunting or chasing or anything of those overwhelming urges that had taught Caine to fear it, that would remind him how dangerous it was. It would be the evidence he needed to stay far, far away from Meaghan.

But it only whined again.

She hates us, it whimpered. *Stay away.*

Caine's heart felt hollow. Even his hellhound had given up.

Something buzzed in his pocket. It took him a moment to recognize it as his phone, and another to realize what it meant.

He fumbled it out of his pocket and swore. With his gloves on he could hardly hold the phone, let alone answer it.

The name on the caller ID made his heart leap. Angus Parker.

When Angus hadn't returned his call, Caine had given up hope that his old friend wanted anything to do with him. Worse, he'd feared Angus was suffering under the same curse as him—and that it was Caine's fault.

But now he was calling back and if Caine could just get his damned gloves off in time to—

The call cut off just as he dropped one glove and tried to swipe to answer it. Caine swore under his breath and tried to call back, but it went straight to voicemail.

Caine tried to be patient. He watched his phone like a hawk, waiting for another call. When his phone buzzed again, though, it was with a series of text messages.

Caine! Buddy! Long time no see. Figured you were off on some self-discovery bullshit after you disappeared. What was it? Mexico? Thailand? Can't wait to hear all about it!

Caine breathed a sigh of relief. That was the Angus he remembered. Always positive.

And... unless he was trying to keep it off the written record, there was no sign he remembered that Caine had transformed into a monstrous hellhound and attacked him. Caine's gut twisted with guilt at the relief he felt.

His phone buzzed again.

Your desk's still waiting for you back here. Hope you're not expecting back pay for your surprise sabbatical though. That last case you were on fell through after you disappeared. You wouldn't recognize that neighborhood if you walked through it now!

A pit formed in Caine's stomach.

That case had been *done*. He'd gathered all the information he needed for his clients to take the property sharks who'd preyed on them to court. And more.

The clients were a group of homeowners who claimed they'd been scammed by a property developer. Angus had thought they were just angry at getting a poor deal, and he'd tossed the case to Caine to sort out.

What Caine had discovered had been almost impressive, if you'd been the sort of person to be impressed by rich assholes lying, threatening, and cheating hard-working families out of everything they owned.

He'd been obsessed with taking them down. Especially once he discovered that this wasn't the first neighborhood that had been targeted in this way.

I had everything we needed to take them down. What happened?

Bitterness flooded Caine's mouth. What sort of a question was that? His hellhound had happened.

He'd attacked Angus. Even if Angus had rationalized the attack away as a hallucination, he wouldn't have been up to taking over Caine's abandoned case. And Caine had disappeared.

He had let his clients down.

I won't let that happen here.

A few minutes ago, Caine had asked himself what he was meant to do now. Well, now he knew. The people of Pine Valley were under attack, the same as his clients had been under attack last Christmas. Except while they were being targeted by property sharks, Pine Valley's enemy was a pack of monsters.

Caine wouldn't risk getting his hellhound involved. But this sort of thing used to be his bread and butter, damn it. And he knew that to stop the hellhounds from attacking Pine Valley, he'd have to find out why they were here in the first place.

He stood up, determination giving him an energy he thought he'd lost when he lost Meaghan. As he regained his bearings, he caught sight of something under the snow.

It looked like a mailbox.

Meaghan said something the Puppy Express delivering letters by dogsled.

The memory made his chest ache, but he couldn't stop himself from walking over and brushing snow off the top of the box. As though touching it would bring him closer to her.

There were two boxes. One mailbox, and one crate that he opened to find a pile of postcards and ballpoint pens wrapped in a waterproof sack. Caine rifled through them. The cards were all Christmas-themed, which made sense; he flicked past almost painfully jolly pictures of Santas, dancing Christmas trees, and elves who were probably going to be nursing a hangover the next day. Then one picture jumped out at him and he stopped.

This postcard was more obviously Puppy Express branded than the others. The front of the postcard had a picture of a dogsled team. The dogs were dressed up for Christmas, with glowing red noses and reindeer antlers. A glittery message read:

This Christmas, send your love by the Puppy Express!

Caine's heart lodged in his throat. He tried to swallow it down, and his eyes watered. He squeezed them tight as his hellhound howled.

Then his eyes sprang open. His hellhound was miserable. He was miserable. He was letting Meaghan think he'd abandoned her and he couldn't risk seeing her, not while his hellhound was still lurking just behind his eyes... but a postcard?

I can't let her leave without knowing how I feel. And that I'm doing all of this, investigating the hellhounds... for her.

He grabbed a pen and wrote a few words that tore at his heart. By the time he finished, his pulse was racing and his bones felt hollow, as though he'd wrung out his soul onto the page.

Caine thrust the card into the mailbox before he could change his mind. Then he spun on his heel and spent the walk back to the Puppy Express building telling himself over and over what a bad idea it had been.

It wasn't until later that he realized he'd not only read Angus' messages without setting his hellhound off, but replied as well. When he did think of it, he thought it was a good thing.

His hellhound was getting weaker. Maybe, by the time he'd solved the mystery of the hellhounds attacked Pine Valley, it would be gone for good.

CHAPTER TWENTY

Meaghan

CHRISTMAS EVE

This isn't so bad, Meaghan lied to herself. *The ghost gang haven't done anything since they ran off with the Santa sleigh. There's even a few last-minute visitors around—a corporate group instead of happy families, sure, but they've got money to burn. Or credit cards, at least. Bob's stopped going pale every time he looks at the Puppy Express bank books.*

Maybe Christmas isn't ruined after all.

Or not for everyone.

Just you.

She was sitting in the Puppy Express dog truck. Her bus ticket was burning a hole in her pocket. One person, one-way. No long goodbyes and no looking back, just her and a backpack of clothes and another town on the horizon that had no idea what was about to hit them.

She was selling her own truck. She wanted to make it as hard as possible for her to come back to Pine Valley, just in case she lost her mind and wanted to come back.

"Meaghan!"

Meaghan jumped and put a protective hand over her jacket pocket as Olly called out to her. "Yeah?"

"We're ready for the dogs now!"

"Okay!"

Olly and Bob, and half the town's business owners and community groups, were gathered in a parking lot on the outskirts of town to prepare for that evening's Santa parade. Since Pine Valley was a small, rural town, most of the "floats" were decorated trucks or snowmobiles. The Puppy Express Santa sleigh was going to bring up the rear, with Bob dressed as Santa Claus and Olly dressed up as one of his elves.

Meaghan had had to reevaluate her idea of Olly as "chill". Over the last two days, she'd been dragged out to check every inch of the route the parade would take into town.

Just in case, Olly had said. In case of what, Meaghan wasn't entirely clear. It wasn't like the ghost gang had raised their heads; and they wouldn't dare attack the parade, anyway. Their whole thing was scaring people while they were on their own and vulnerable, and the whole town was going to show up for the Santa parade. Everyone who hadn't decided to spend the holiday elsewhere, anyway.

The air outside was crisp. Meaghan breathed it in. One thing she would miss about Pine Valley—okay, one of many—was the fresh air. And the way the stars stretched all the way across the sky on clear nights.

"And you too, doofuses," she cooed as she trudged to the back of the truck and let the dogs out of their boxes one by one. "Come on. Let's get you kitted up and on the sleigh."

She knew she was going to miss almost everything about this

place, and its people. But it wasn't enough to make her stay. Not when every breath of crisp air, or glimmer of starlight, or goofy doggy grin reminded her of Caine.

First, though, she had to get through the Santa parade.

"What do you think?" Olly pushed her way through the mob of dogs and did a quick twirl.

"Very Christmassy." Olly was wearing a short green tunic with white fuzzy trim, candy-striped stockings and a red hat with a pom-pom on the end. To Meaghan's surprise, given how stressed she'd been about the parade route, Olly was smiling.

"What about you? I hope you've got some party clothes on under than coat. Or… maybe you have other plans for after the parade?"

It was impossible to miss the hope in Olly's voice. Meaghan bit back a sigh. Olly wasn't just convinced that Meaghan was going to storm up the mountain and bully Caine into taking her back; she seemed to think that Meaghan and Caine getting together would somehow make up for her and Jackson not working out.

Meaghan didn't have the heart to tell her that not only was she not planning to storm up anywhere, she was leaving town.

"I've got plans, yeah," she said, which didn't really count as a lie. It was just that her plans involved packing her running-away bag, not chasing down true love. "What about you? Are you going to the Heartwell party?"

"Pine Valley's biggest shifter Christmas party? A few days after I broke a poor non-shifter-boy's heart?" Olly's smile dropped. "I have to help Uncle Bob with the Puppy Express deliveries. And after that… I don't know. Jackson might be there…"

"You shouldn't let that ruin Christmas for you."

"I know." Olly pulled herself up. "I should take a leaf out of your book, right? Not let anything get me down."

God no. "Uh, sure."

"Will you bring Caine?"

Meaghan's head spun. "Uh, I think I—have you got the dog costumes?"

Olly swore and hurried away. Meaghan watched her go, waiting until she was out of sight before she sagged back against the side of her truck.

She hated lying to Olly. But what else could she do? If she told Olly the truth about why she wouldn't, *couldn't*, go after Caine…

Meaghan gulped. She always pushed. She always pushed until whatever tolerance people had for her broke, and then she picked up the pieces and moved on and it didn't matter that they wanted her gone, because she'd made it happen. They didn't want her because of something she'd *done*. Not because of who she was.

And that was why Caine's horror at the thought of being with her was a line she couldn't cross. If she left, she could keep pretending that it was all a mistake. Just a really, really bad hookup.

If she confronted Caine, and it was all true, then her worst fears would come true. All those sneaky, scared thoughts that had chased her through foster care, when foster home after foster home hadn't worked out.

No one could ever love you.

Except it was even worse than that.

Only a monster could love you.

CHAPTER TWENTY-ONE

Caine

Caine staggered. The Christmas lights that filled the town square seemed to dim. Caine's breath caught in his throat—but this wasn't his hellhound.

The darkness at the edges of his vision wasn't smoke. Just the shadows of exhaustion. He leaned against the nearest tree and closed his eyes.

Not yet, huh, Hellhound? You're sticking around for a bit longer?

There was no reply. Caine's thoughts echoed in his head, cold and empty.

His hellhound had grown weaker every day. Which was lucky, because Caine was weakening, too. There was no way he'd be able to help move any trees now. Let alone stop his hellhound from wreaking havoc if it tried to escape.

But it hadn't. Not since it had decided that the reason Meaghan had left was that she hated it. It just stayed curled up in the deepest shadows of his heart, wrapped around that strange, flickering golden light as though it was the most important thing in the world.

More important than chasing down innocent people? he thought bitterly. *More important than—*

"—Work needed, of course, but with *potential*. Like I told you in July—"

All of Caine's senses went on high alert.

He knew that voice. The last time he'd heard it, it had been raised in fear and anger.

Angus Parker.

What the hell is he doing here?

Caine knew he should go and talk to his old friend, but instead, he almost tripped over his own feet in his haste to hide deeper in the shadows under the Christmas trees. The last time his hellhound had seen Angus, it had tried to tear his throat out. It hadn't reacted to him exchanging text messages with him but if it noticed him now, in the flesh...

He held his breath as Angus strode into view. He was deep in conversation with a solidly built, gray-haired man who looked like he was hanging off his every word.

"Back in July when I told you to go to hell?" the older man sighed. Angus burst out laughing and clapped him on the back.

"All forgotten, buddy. Trust me, in my line of work, that's basically 'hello'."

"Ever since the fire..." The older man licked his lips unhappily. "If the price you were talking about back in July is still on the table..."

"I'm sure we'll come to an arrangement that pleases us both. Let's talk over dinner," Angus said grandly.

Caine frowned. *That's Mr. Bell. The one who owns the store that burnt down. Is Angus trying to buy it? But since when is he interested in commercial real estate?*

The conversation was setting off alarm bells in Caine's head, and it took him a moment to figure out why.

Of course. It was all too familiar. The same sort of thing Caine had been investigating before the attack. In that scam, a cartel had targeted neighborhoods one by one. They'd sent in "investors" to talk to locals about what great prices they could offer for their houses, most of whom had been laughed out of the street by people with no wish to sell their family homes or businesses.

Then things had started to go wrong. Power outages. Broken pipes. Maybe a fire or two but somehow, always things that weren't covered by insurance. Enough accidents so that by the next time the "investors" came around, the locals needed money bad, even if the price they were being offered was a lot lower than the first time around.

It's too close. Too similar. Too...

Angus turned and for a moment, Caine thought he'd spoken out loud. Inside him, his hellhound bared its teeth.

Him! it snarled. Caine braced himself, ready to fend off an attack which never came. Instead, his hellhound backed deeper into the shadows of his soul, curling its whole body around the strange golden light as though it was trying to keep it from Angus' sight.

Angus stared into the trees. There shouldn't have been any way he could miss Caine standing there. But his gaze went straight through him.

He shrugged and looked away and Caine sagged, exhausted. He waited until Angus was out of sight and then slunk away from the trees he'd hidden under. Strings of lights caught on his sleeves and his hands shook as he untangled them. Strange; he hadn't noticed walking into them when he stepped under the trees...

Angus was across the square, heading for the Grill. Snatches of his conversation reached Caine's ears but it was his other senses that were suddenly on edge.

His hellhound's senses.

Nothing had changed; the square was still filling slowly with people, mostly locals by the look of them, but a few unfamiliar faces that must be the corporate group Hank had mentioned.

False hope. The hairs on the backs of Caine's arms prickled. *Why did I just think that?*

He sifted through his memories again and remembered what he'd written about the scam he'd been investigating last Christmas.

Step one. The cartel raises price expectations by sending in fake investors to seed the idea of big returns in locals' minds.

Step two. Make life hell. The more debt the locals get into trying to fix up the "accidents" the cartel arranged, the better. Make them desperate.

Step three. False hope. A miracle from above. The investors are back, and the offer's still good. But then…

Ice ran down Caine's spine.

He didn't know what Angus' part in all of this was, but something was very wrong. He could map everything that had happened in Pine Valley onto the scam he'd been so close to solving.

Only whoever was behind this scam wasn't using sewage leaks and power outages to kill local business and sow desperation. They were using hellhounds.

And the next step in the scam—

He broke into a run.

I have to find Meaghan.

CHAPTER TWENTY-TWO

Meaghan

"Is Bob around?" Meaghan asked. She checked her watch. "It's almost time to get started. Everyone else is in position."

Olly looked vague. It was the expression she always got when she was communicating with telepathy. "He's just finishing curling his beard. He'll be a minute. Besides, we don't need to start moving until after everyone else."

"He's curling his beard?"

Olly shrugged. "He takes it *very* seriously."

Meaghan raised her eyebrows. "Right…"

At least everything else is ready, she thought. Olly looked great, so long as she remembered to smile instead of peering intently at people.

The dogs were all dressed up in their reindeer outfits. Each of them was wearing a snow jacket with a pair of antlers on the hood and tiny silver bells jingling from stitched-on saddles. Parkour, as lead dog, had a kitten plushie attached to his "saddle". Meaghan wasn't sure why, but Jasper Heartwell had begged for it to be included, and Parkour was fine with it.

And being dog-napped by the ghost gang doesn't seem to have had any lasting effects. Except for Parkour growling at that corporate group yesterday. But he's always a bit of a nut.

She knelt down and scratched Parkour's ears. All six dogs were tail-waggingly cheerful and ready to go.

They're as happy to see me as when... ugh.

When she first met Caine. Why did she have to think about that now?

The moment the thought crossed her mind, all six sled dogs went still and alert. Meaghan's skin tingled.

Just like when they first saw him.

She looked up, and there he was. Across the other side of the car park. Far enough away that she shouldn't have been able to tell it was him. Not so quickly or with such absolute, heart-thudding certainty.

Shit. What am I supposed to do now?

She shook herself. What was she thinking? There was no way he was here to see her. *He doesn't want anything to do with you, remember?*

He must want to see Bob, or Hank, or…

Except…

Caine was walking straight past all the other lined-up parade floats. Right towards the sleigh. Either he was really keen to catch up with the dogs, or…

Meaghan gulped. He *was* coming to see her.

That tiny golden spark of hope flared up in her heart. She rubbed her chest.

Calm down. Calm down. Even if he is going to see you, he's not going to…

She sighed and closed her eyes. If Christmas wishes were real, he would be coming to tell her *he* loved her, not his hellhound, and he wanted to be with her, and they would ride into town on the Santa sleigh with people cheering them on, straight into their happy ever after.

Caine's gravelly voice broke through her daydream.

"Meaghan, you have to get out of here."

Meaghan's eyes shot open. "What?"

The daydream shattered.

Caine must have run across the parking lot. He was standing on the other side of the sleigh, exhaustion in every line of his body and red spots of exertion on his pale cheeks.

"You have to leave. Now. Something's—"

Meaghan's ears filled with the roar of blood.

"You came all the way over here to tell me that I have to *leave?*"

Olly squeaked. Caine took a half-step backwards, his eyebrows drawing together.

"Yes, but—"

"I'm already leaving! Isn't that good enough? Just two more days and you'll be rid of me forever!"

"That's not what I—"

"Shut up! Just stop talking!"

Caine's mouth snapped shut. Meaghan leaned on the side of the sleigh, panting.

Hot and cold shivers goose-bumped down her skin and she was worried she was going to be sick.

He doesn't just want nothing to do with you. He wants you gone.

His hellhound is a monster. And he's finally figured out that means you're a monster, too.

Tears filled her eyes. "This is why I never wanted to see you again!" she cried out, her voice hoarse.

That golden spark inside her flickered like a candle in the breeze.

Caine hissed in a breath and clutched at his chest. Meaghan

clambered onto the sleigh and just managed to stop herself from tumbling off the other side and into his arms.

He doesn't want you, remember?

Too big. Too loud. Too unlovable.

Monster.

Somewhere on the edges of her panicked rage, the dogs began to howl.

Caine's eyes went wide. His mouth twisted, but stayed shut, as though it was stuck together with invisible superglue.

"I had to be an idiot to think I'd finally found someone who liked me, right? You think your hellhound's a disgusting monster and I am too! Just admit it!"

Meaghan's eyes blurred, but the wind whipped away her tears before they fell.

Caine opened his mouth with a gasp. "If it wasn't for my hellhound I would never leave you!"

"Bullshit!" Meaghan had to scream over the howling wind. "You're lying!"

"I'm not—" Caine's voice wavered.

"Meaghan!" Olly shrieked. "They're here!"

Meaghan's head snapped around. "What?"

"Look!"

Meaghan followed her shaking finger. "I don't see—oh God."

The noise of the wind and the parade preparations fell away, and the silence that pressed in on her was unnatural. It was as though the world was blanketed in thick fog and snow.

Three huge shadowy hounds flickered in and out of sight at the edges of the parking lot. Their legs were long and rangy, their heads held low. Hellfire burned in their eyes and smoke coiled out of their panting jaws.

Panic gnawed at her insides just at the sight of them. The same panic that had made her admit all her worst fears to Caine.

"Hellhounds," Meaghan whispered. Her own voice sounded strange and thin in her ears.

As soon as she spoke, they vanished. She looked around desperately. There was no trace of them. But the unnatural silence hadn't lifted.

Caine grabbed her arm. "Please," he said, his voice rough. "This is why I came. I've seen all this before. Not exactly the same, but—they're going to do something. I need you to be safe."

He took a step backwards and Meaghan moved with him, stepping off the sleigh.

"What do you mean, you know what they're doing?"

Caine's face was strained. "I think—"

Olly's shriek cut through the air. Meaghan twisted out of Caine's grasp as the sled dogs began to howl again.

And run.

Olly thudded back against the seat as the sleigh burst into motion. Meaghan didn't stop to think. She leapt onto the sleigh beside her.

"*Mmf.*" She gasped, winded. "Olly, can you—Olly?"

Olly was crouched in the very corner of the seat, her eyes wide.

Meaghan gulped. *If I'm terrified, how must she feel? She said looking into their eyes was like having your brain scraped out until it was only the bad memories left, and her bad memories with Jackson are so close.*

She reached out to grab Olly's hand and turned back to the dogs.

"Whoa!" she shouted. The wind tore her voice away. "I said *Whoa!*"

The dogs didn't listen. Or maybe they didn't hear. Or maybe...

A shiver clutched at Meaghan's spine and she looked slowly to her left.

Burning eyes sneered back at her.

Nobody wants you. Nobody ever wanted you. And it's all your fault. Everything is.

She sat down hard.

The hellhounds are driving the dogs. But where? And why are they doing this?

"Meaghan!"

Caine's voice thundered through her bones. She twisted around in time to see him grab the side of the sleigh and brace himself to slow it. Wood splintered under his fingers and the sleigh raced on.

"Grab my hand!" Meaghan yelled, reaching for him.

His hand closed around hers and he vaulted onto the sleigh. It rocked under his extra weight and Meaghan tensed.

Caine met her eyes. A flicker of understanding passed between them. "We can't let the sleigh turn over. They won't stop."

Meaghan swallowed. "They won't let the dogs stop even if their leads get tangled? They'll get hurt!"

"I was thinking more along the lines of *us* getting hurt."

"But we have to do something!"

Beside her, Olly moaned. "No, no, no..." Her hands were pressed up against her face. As Meaghan watched, feathers sprouted between her fingers. "No no *no...*"

"Whatever they're doing to the dogs is affecting her as well," Caine groaned. Meaghan's attention whiplashed from Olly, to him. His face was creased with pain.

"And you?"

"I can... manage it."

It was affecting her, as well. Adrenaline was rushing through her system. She gulped.

"They're driving us towards the town."

What was it Opal had said? *Scared people make stupid decisions.*

"Those streets will be full of people."

"Don't let them see me like this!" Olly cried. "I can't stop it—"

The streets had been plowed that morning. Huge drifts of snow were piled up either side of the road. But only here. The closer they got to town, the less snow there would be.

Meaghan saw her chance and made a split-second decision. She grabbed Olly's hand and pulled her upright as the sleigh neared a corner.

"Jump!" she yelled. Olly squeaked and leapt into the drift at the side of the road.

"That's her safe. What about you?" Caine's voice was hoarse. Meaghan turned to him, her eyes flashing.

"You mean *us*," she snapped. The candlelight-spark inside her flared.

"I have to keep you safe. That's the only thing that's important anymore." Caine groaned and clutched his head.

Meaghan pulled him down beside her. Wisps of tinsel were flying off the sleigh, and wood and steel creaked beneath her.

"We're almost in town. And the sleigh isn't going to hold up much longer at this speed. We have to slow them down somehow."

"No more snowdrifts," Caine gritted out, wincing.

Of course. That must have been what stopped their last joyride. I should have crashed us all into that last snowdrift, not just Olly.

You thought you could save Christmas? You can't even save yourself.

They were at the edge of town now, on the long straight street that led to the square. Surprised shouts and the occasional whoop of excitement filtered through the howling silence from the people waiting for the parade only a few dozen yards away.

The sled dogs were panting, their eyes rolling in their heads. Meaghan gritted her teeth.

"There has to be something we can do to stop them!"

Windows shattered as the hellhounds, little more than shadows streaming smoke and sparks, stalked the streets.

The sled jolted on a pothole and Caine put his arm around her and pressed his face close to hers.

"This is what I wanted to keep you safe from. Look around you. Do you see what I am now? The truth? Hellhounds are monsters." His voice was wracked with misery. "I'm one of them. I can feel it in my bones. Their hunt is calling to me, and I can't—I have to fight it, but..."

He cursed and dropped his head against hers. His next words were a whisper, barely audible. "I have to get you out of here before you get hurt. That's all I wanted. You're not a monster, you're—you're perfect. And I don't deserve to be with you so long as I'm one of *them*."

Meaghan felt as though she'd run headlong into a wall.

It's not just his hellhound. It's him. He cares about me. Caine cares about me.

Acid whispers crawled into the corners of her brain. Wrong. Wrong! You think that's the truth? No one could ever care about a creature like you. Remember falling off that wall? Remember all the families that gave up on you because you were never good enough, no matter how hard you tried?

She squeezed her eyes shut. "No..."

It's because you'll NEVER be good enough. You're broken inside. Worthless. Unworthy of love. All you can do is destroy things.

Only a monster could love you. Don't you think you should let Caine go before you destroy him, too?

Meaghan's eyes flew open.

That wasn't her. It was someone else. Someone with a voice like acid knives, speaking inside her head.

She grabbed Caine's head between her hands, forcing him to look at her.

"I've been wrong about everything," she gasped. "I think. I hope. Oh, God, Caine, what if we both have been?"

"Meaghan, what are you talking about?"

"Your hellhound. It's not a monster."

Caine's eyes widened. "You can't know that—"

She didn't have time to explain. She didn't know how she would have explained it, either. She would have sounded like a crazy woman. *An evil voice in my head told me all the things I am most afraid of are true—so I knew they weren't?*

It was insane. Ridiculous.

Just like when she'd been convinced there was more behind the weird shit going on in Pine Valley than just coincidences.

And she'd been right then. Not wrong. Not screwing things up. *Right.*

NO!!!

"Caine, I love you," she screamed over the acid voice screaming in her head, and kissed him.

CHAPTER TWENTY-THREE

Caine

Meaghan's lips melted against his, hot as the fire blazing in his heart. Caine's hellhound sang, its eyes reflecting the perfect bright light it had been protecting ever since Meaghan left him. She was back now, and that tiny candlelight was burning as huge and golden as the sun.

Meaghan loved him. She wanted him. *All* of him. And he—

She gasped against his lips as the golden light in his heart flared. "What was that? It felt like—"

Brakes squealed just ahead of the sleigh. The dogs screamed as the sleigh shunted sideways. Meaghan slipped out of Caine's grasp, hurtling directly towards the four-wheel drive that had appeared out of nowhere—

And Caine let go of every mental control he had spent the last twelve months constructing.

The hellhound ripped out of him. Muscled legs. Razor-sharp claws. Teeth that dripped smoke and eyes like gateways to Hell itself.

It was a monstrous, terrifying beast. And it wasn't going to let anyone hurt the woman he loved.

Caine twisted in the air, leaping between Meaghan and the car. He curled around her as she hit his side, trying to cushion her landing as much as possible.

The *oof* of breath she let out as she hit him *hurt*. The hellhound shivered.

Is she safe? Is she injured?

Meaghan stood up slowly, swearing under her breath.

She's fine, Caine reassured his trembling hellhound.

Meaghan's eyes widened as she looked at him.

"Caine?" she breathed. "This is incredible. You're so—so…"

Caine knew what she was seeing. A huge, rangy, wolf-like creature that looked like something from a nightmare. He held his breath with his hellhound.

She reached out and gently touched his muzzle. A bright sort of shiver went through her, traveling through her hand into Caine's body and lodging in the golden sun in his heart. His veins sang with wonder.

"If I'd seen you like this three days ago, I never would have thought you were a monster," she said, and hugged him around his massive neck. "I've wasted so much time being so stupid and *sad*."

Her tangled emotions surged through the connection between them. Caine's hellhound whined and tried to nuzzle her, and he reached out along the connection and found another well of golden sun at the end of it. Meaghan's heart. He sent all his love down it, and his regret at letting her stay in pain so long. And his promise that it would never happen again.

She gasped. "That was like when we kissed. What is it?"

Caine's hellhound grumbled something and she laughed. "I don't know why I'm asking questions. It's not like you can answer me like this."

We can't speak telepathically? All my migraines—but that was when I hated my hellhound. If I wasn't so focused on locking away everything about it...

No sooner had he thought the words than something released in Caine's mind. A moment later, a voice blasted into his mind.

What's happening down there?

Caine's hellhound yelped. That was Jasper's voice—Jasper's dragon, calling into his mind like fireworks. And he could hear him. And it didn't hurt.

Could he call back?

"Maybe you can't talk to me, but I bet you can *hear* me," Meaghan said. She put her hands either side of his hellhound's massive head. Her expression was so fierce and determined it made Caine's heart sing along with his hellhound's. "We have to stop the other hellhounds. Are you with me?"

Caine and his hellhound took a deep breath. Pine Valley was under attack. All hell was breaking loose.

And his mate needed him. Caine barked his agreement and shouted silently:

What's happening? We're going to save Christmas.

Could Jasper hear him? Could Meaghan? It didn't matter. She grinned at him, and her faith in him—in him not being a monster—burst into his heart like the first sunrise at midwinter.

The hellhounds had run ahead. He could hear them baying and howling as they turned their attention from the dogs to the people lining the streets for the Santa parade.

He knelt so Meaghan could climb on his back, and they ran to the town center.

The square was in chaos. Lights and Christmas displays had been dragged down. Windows were smashed. People were screaming. And the hellhounds...

The hellhounds were in chaos, too. Caine sniffed the air.

His senses were sharper in this form. Not just the usual ones, but something else, as well. It was as though he could smell, or hear, or see or feel, *power.*

This new power-sense told him the hellhounds were following orders, but the orders were wild and undirected, and *wrong.* The hellhounds were obeying a command so strong that it vibrated through the air, but it wasn't the *right* command.

Caine's hellhound growled uneasily. *I know,* he told it. *Something isn't right here. We need to stop them. And stop whoever's telling them to do this.*

Caine? Jasper's voice lit up his mind again. *There's not enough room for me to land down there. I'll find somewhere to shift. Can you handle things until backup arrives?*

I'll do my best, Caine called back.

Meaghan sat astride his shoulders, gripping his mane-like hair like she was holding reins.

"There!" she yelled. "By the eggnog truck!"

The food truck Caine had seen his first evening with Meaghan was open for the parade. One of the hellhounds was stalking toward it.

Caine leapt in front of it.

Villain! his hellhound growled, snapping its teeth.

The hellhound hesitated, one paw off the ground. *Who are you? Why do you smell so familiar?*

Why are you attacking innocent people? Caine sniffed the air. The hellhound was smaller than him, and so thin its ribs showed. Caine's new sixth sense showed him the strange power of command wrapped around him like chains. His hellhound snarled. *Who's making you do this?*

The hellhound snapped back. *Who else? The alpha! Can't you*

197

hear him?

Caine frowned and strained his senses. The hellhound leapt for his throat.

Caine's hellhound's reflexes saved him. It darted to the side, smacking the other shifter to the ground with one heavy paw. The hellhound grunted and staggered to its feet.

The command that wrapped around the hellhound was so strong it made Caine's teeth ache. It whimpered and crept forward, fangs bared.

It doesn't want to do this, Caine realized. *This "alpha" is forcing them to fight for it.*

Want or not, the hellhound was obeying. Its muscles bunched to leap at him again.

"Down!" Meaghan's voice rang like a bell. "Stay there! Bad dog!"

The hellhound flattened itself against the ground, whimpering. Caine twisted his head to stare at Meaghan in amazement.

The light from his fiery eyes danced on her skin as she shrugged, biting her lower lip.

"I thought—well, *you* seem to do what you're told when I'm the one doing the telling..."

Caine and his hellhound huffed in simultaneous displeasure, and then Caine laughed silently. His hellhound didn't want Meaghan giving orders to anyone but *him.*

They took down the other two hellhounds in quick succession. Meaghan didn't even need to order the third one down; one look at Caine and it slunk away with its ears down.

The vibration of command in the air changed. The alpha was losing control. The power it wielded like a chain around the other hellhound's necks was weakening.

And it was angry.

Which means it's time to take the fight to him.

Get the humans out of here, he called to anyone who was listening. Across the square, Hannah was already ushering people into her restaurant. Caine stared up into the sky. It was full of stars—but no dragons.

Meaghan leaned forward and whispered in Caine's ear: "Let's finish this before anyone gets hurt."

The alpha. Caine's new sense was blazing. That vibration of command, the thrum of power and hierarchy... it all led back to one point. One *leash*.

Caine swung his head around, searching the crowds for the face he knew had to be there. It all made sense now.

Figured it out, have you?

Caine went completely still.

Angus was seated at the same table he and Meaghan had eaten at, overlooking the square, the Heartwell Christmas Forest... and all the destruction he'd brought down on the town.

Caine's hellhound bared its teeth. *You.*

"Mr. Parker?" Caine could feel Meaghan standing to peer over his head. "The investor?"

Questions Caine had given up even finding an answer to slotted into place.

Like why he'd been attacked last year in the first place.

His stomach curdled. Angus was the one who put him onto the property development case in the first place. He'd bet him he couldn't crack the scam.

It was you all along. Caine walked across the square. Every step seemed to take all the energy he had. *Were you behind that first scam, too, or did you just see what I discovered and see a chance to use your shifter powers to make some money?* He bared his teeth. *Our business was meant to help people, not find new ways to hurt*

199

them!

The private investigator racket? Angus' telepathic laughter sent shivers down Caine's spine. *There's a limit to the amount of money I could blackmail out of our clients without you noticing. Whereas this...*

He spread his arms.

Do you know how many small towns like this there are across America, just waiting to be scooped up? The shifters here were stupid. Too afraid of revealing their true selves to defend their own town. They don't understand just how hard humans will try to ignore the evidence of their own eyes. Tomorrow, no one here will want to admit to anyone that they thought they saw ghostly hounds attack the town. They'll just tell themselves they imagined it, and go home, and worry about how they're going to afford to fix all the damage.

I won't let you do this. Caine was beneath the balcony now. He squared off against his old friend as Angus lounged on the balcony rail, smiling easily. *Come down here and let's talk. If you're doing this because of money troubles again, we can sort something out—*

Money troubles? The only money trouble I have is other people having what I deserve! Angus' smile dropped off his face and then returned, narrow and sly. *You don't remember, do you?*

Remember what?

Meaghan leaned over his shoulder. "Caine, what's going on?" she whispered in his ear.

Angus' sly grin widened, and Caine's feeling of unease grew. *Something is very wrong here. What don't I remember?*

You want to stop me, Boy Scout? Go on. Try.

I don't want to hurt you, Angus.

Oh, big surprise there. You always were too soft.

But he's the one behind all of this, Caine thought. *He might have been my friend, once, but now he's hurting people.*

The balcony behind Angus was empty now. He was the only person on the Grill's rooftop.

Caine bunched his muscles and leapt.

"Stop!" Angus barked out loud. Caine's muscles spasmed. He collapsed to the ground.

And Angus' command wove chains around him.

Angus spread his hands on the railing, staring down at him with utter contempt. "You did forget, didn't you?" he remarked, raising one eyebrow. "I'm the one who made you like this, Caine. I knew you'd cracked the case, and I needed to make sure you weren't going to take it to the authorities."

Meaghan gasped. Caine's claws scrabbled on the icy cobblestones.

The chase. That first hunt. That was him.

No wonder he looked so shocked when he found me in the office the next morning.

Caine's horror must have flooded out through his telepathic abilities. Meaghan clenched her hands in his fur. "What's wrong?" she whispered, her voice trembling. "Caine, can you hear me?"

"He can hear you, whoever you are," Angus drawled. "He's just a bit busy remembering who he really is."

You bit me and you left me for dead. Caine's telepathic voice shook **That's why my hellhound attacked you the next morning.**

"You remember how that ended up, Boy Scout?"

The hunt. There were two hunts, after all. When he attacked me—and when I attacked him.

This time's going to be different.

"You really think that? This isn't a contract job, Boy Scout. It's for life. Sure, I've been a generous boss and let you out on sabbatical for a year, but it's time you came back into the fold. I made you. You're part of my pack. Now *heel.*"

The command tugged at Caine's bones. He lowered his head, snarling.

No!

Angus' face twisted. "Get to work!"

Spread fear. Spread terror. Be the shadow at the corner of their eye, the noise in the night. Make them afraid to leave their houses.

"Leave him alone!"

Caine twisted his head around. Meaghan was standing on his back, glaring up at Angus.

"I don't know who the hell you think you are, asshole, but if you think Caine's going to do anything you say—"

"He doesn't have a choice." Angus' eyes narrowed. "I know you, don't I? That twisted, scared little mind. You should have left when I told you to."

Order me to fight him, Caine begged silently, hoping against hope that Meaghan could hear him. He focused all his energy on the burning golden sun inside him, and the connection to the light in Meaghan's heart. *You know I'll do anything you command. Your command, not his.*

Caine? Is that you?

Meaghan!

Meaghan's telepathic voice was as fierce and wonderful as her speaking voice. *I'm not going to order you to do anything,* she said firmly. She repeated it out loud, glaring at Angus.

"Hah!" Angus barked a single burst of laughter. "You're both weak. What are you planning to do, you stupid girl, ask him nicely? He's a hellhound. He only responds to force!"

"I don't think that's true." Meaghan's voice rang like a bell in Caine's head and his heart.

"Have it your way. You ask him nicely, and I'll order him...

202

and we'll see who his real boss is."

Meaghan, no!

Angus' alpha power pressed against his mind like a black cloud. Caine fought it off, but the alpha's chains tightened around him, as strong and relentless as the chains he'd used to bind his own hellhound.

Meaghan, please, he begged, and then he felt her hand on his head, soft and gentle.

Don't worry, Caine. I'm not going to screw up. Not this time. She kissed the top of his head and sat back down on his shoulders. *Now—*

Angus bared his teeth. *Attack—*

Let's take him down. Together.

Meaghan's voice washed over Caine like cool water. The chains melted away. Up on the balcony, Angus' face twisted with rage and confusion.

He stumbled back as Caine leapt onto the balcony. Fire poured from his eyes, but Caine knocked him back and held him down with one paw.

I wouldn't do that if I were you. You might have won the last time we fought, but this time, I'm not alone.

He focused on the mate-bond that ran like a golden rope between him and Meaghan, knowing that she would be able to hear him.

This time, I have my mate with me. And if she decides to stop playing nice? You're going to have a very, very bad time.

Caine felt the moment Angus' hellhound yielded. The tangled web of power that forced his pack to attack innocent people dissolved, and Caine's hellhound felt freer than it ever had before.

Free... and not dangerous. Not to Meaghan and not to anyone else. Caine knew now how wrong he'd been about it. It had never been evil—just trying to help.

"With its teeth," Meaghan muttered, and laughed. "Better than a dead mouse, but still…"

What? Caine didn't think he'd telepathed at her, but maybe their ability to communicate through the mate-bond wasn't telepathy after all. Maybe it was something special. Something *theirs*.

"I'll explain later." Meaghan slid off his back and tossed a disdainful look at Angus.

The other hellhound shifter was lying in a bedraggled heap. He was still conscious, and the look of hatred he shot at Meaghan and Caine was almost enough to make Caine want to go another round with him.

But Angus wasn't just on the ground. He was *defeated*. Caine's hellhound smirked.

He doesn't have power over anyone anymore, it explained to Caine. *His hellhound knows who the alpha is now. The human couldn't fight you if he tried.*

Who the alpha is now? Caine was still puzzling over that one when Meaghan tugged his chin to make him face her.

Her face was shining. "Hello, my love."

Hello. Caine's hellhound nuzzled her and… stepped back. *Your turn now*, it said to Caine.

Shifting this time wasn't painful, or terrifying. It was easy. As soon as he had arms again, Caine swept Meaghan up in them. "Guess what?"

She laughed delightedly. "What?"

"I think you just saved Christmas."

She stared at him, eyes sparkling in the light of a hundred Christmas trees. "Wrong again, my love," she whispered, and her shiver of happiness at calling him *her love* whispered down the mate-bond into his heart. "*We* saved Christmas. And now…" She leaned her face closer to his.

"Now?" He moved closer, until their lips were almost touching.

"Now... you need to find some pants."

CHAPTER TWENTY-FOUR

Meaghan

Pants were the easy part. Explaining what had just happened, to a town of freaked-out humans who had no idea that shifters existed… was also surprisingly easy.

Angus might be an asshole, but he was right about humans not wanting to believe the evidence of their own eyes. Jasper ran into the middle of the square a few minutes after Jackson had snapped the last cuffs on the defeated hellhound shifters, thanked everyone for taking part in the inaugural Heartwell Interactive Christmas Pageant—Meaghan had no idea where he dragged that up from—and everything was fine.

The hard part was going to be getting even a millisecond alone with Caine after the other shifters caught up with them. Before Meaghan knew what was happening, she was squashed in the back of Hank Heartwell's family-sized SUV, heading up the mountains to the Heartwell Christmas Eve party.

She hadn't let go of Caine's hand since he had shifted back into human form. And put on some pants.

The drive up to the Heartwell Lodge seemed to go past in a flash. As they all tumbled out of the car, Opal dove in front of Meaghan and hugged her so hard Meaghan's "Thanks for the ride" came out as a croak.

"I knew you'd sort it out!" Opal beamed at her. "Merry Christmas, both of you. Now let's get inside and have some mulled wine to warm up."

Next, a cannonball that turned out to be a human-shaped Cole thumped onto Caine's back.

"Merry Christmas!" he yelled in both of their ears. "Caine, my dragon wants to meet your hellhound! Can it? Please? Your hellhound is *so cool!*"

"Maybe later," Caine replied, grinning.

"Is there room for another hug in there?" Hank came up behind his wife and nodded at Meaghan. "Hell of a Santa parade, huh? I don't think our party's going to top that."

"You have to tell us everything!" Abigail was running over from her and Jasper's car, followed by Jasper, who was cradling Ruby. "Who was that man Caine stopped? Was he something to do with the hellhound shifters?"

Tension prickled along Meaghan's spine. But it wasn't *her* tension. She looked up at Caine. *Are you all right?*

He squeezed her hand. *With you beside me? Always.*

"And what was he saying, about being inside your mind?"

This time the tension crackling up her spine was *definitely* her own. Oh God. The last thing she wanted to do now was talk about all the ways that evil hellhound had needled into her brain…

Do you need me to scare them off? Caine's voice was the perfect antidote to the memory of those acid words.

Maybe, Meaghan admitted. Caine smiled at her.

It's up to you, he whispered in her mind.

Meaghan bit her lip. All she'd wanted for so long was a Christmas surrounded by people who actually wanted to be around her—and now that it looked like she was going to have one, all she could think about were all the things she would rather do right now than be at a party.

Like make up for the last three days, for a start.

Caine's cheeks colored. *Did you mean to say that out loud?*

Did I what? Eyes wide, Meaghan stared around the gathered shifters. "Oh God. Did everyone hear that?"

"Hear what?" Abigail asked, elbowing her way past the dragon shifters. "Merry Christmas, you two. I'm so happy for you."

I guess not? Caine suggested.

Warmth emanated from the golden light in her heart, filling her whole body. Her cheeks heated up when she realized it was coming from Caine. He was sending her joy, and love, and very inappropriate thoughts along the strange new connection between them.

I think only I can hear you. Because of this. He sent another flood of love along the connection.

Meaghan bit back a smirk. *Does that mean if I think about—*

"Skreeeeark!"

A snowy owl appeared out of the trees, wheeled once around Meaghan and Caine's heads, and landed on the closest tree branch. Meaghan gasped.

"Olly? Is that you?"

Olly's snowy owl was beautiful, with soft white plumage with darker flecks on her chest. She landed on top of Hank's SUV and tipped its head on one side, just like Olly did when she was assessing a situation in human form.

"I can't hear if she's saying anything," Meaghan murmured.

"No, because you're not a shifter." Cole wrinkled his nose and kept talking before Meaghan could explain about being able to talk to Caine inside her head. "But I can't hear her anyway. She isn't talking to me."

Caine let go of her hand, but only so he could wrap his arm around her. He lowered his face to her ear and whispered: "She says, inspecting a situation from all angles is important before you get *into* a situation, but it can also help when you want to get *out*." His eyes warmed. "Do you know what she's talking about?"

"I think so." Meaghan leaned into him. "Tell her thanks from me."

Caine frowned with concentration, and Olly startled, fluttering her wings. "Sorry!" he called out. "I think I need to practice on my telepathy volume."

Olly preened one of her wing feathers and then leapt into the air and flew off. Meaghan waved at her.

You don't have volume problems talking to me,* she reminded him.

That's because you're right here. In my heart. Smoky flames flared in his eyes. *Where you should have been from the start.*

"Well!" said Opal, rubbing her hands together somewhere very far away. "This party won't start itself. Come on, Cole, inside and wash your hands. Jasper, did you remember to…"

The voices faded as the Heartwells headed for the house. Caine started to follow them, but Meaghan dragged her feet.

"Caine…" she murmured, and then again, sending it along the golden thread that connected them, *My love…*

Caine shivered in a way that sent heat flooding through her core. *Yes?*

It was amazing, how easy communicating telepathically with him was. Talking to him like this was like being wrapped in his arms, in some faraway, private world of their own.

I know what Olly meant. About finding the perfect time to disappear. She raised her eyebrows and sent a teasing, highly

209

inappropriate thought down their connection.

Caine's eyes went dark. "Ah."

Do you want to—

Caine cut her off with a kiss that made every inch of her tingle. When he pulled back to breathe, she grabbed his collar and kissed him back. He wrapped his arms around her, one around her waist, the other cradling the back of her head as he deepened the kiss.

Meaghan was trembling by the time their lips parted. Caine was breathing heavily. They both were.

Their eyes met.

"Let's get out of here," Caine murmured.

A thrill went through Meaghan. "How? Steal one of the Heartwells' trucks?"

"I have a better idea." Caine kissed Meaghan's hands. "Thank you for showing me I can trust this part of me."

He took a step back. His skin started to shimmer, then the air twisted around him and the hellhound stood in front of Meaghan.

It lowered its head, stretching out its front legs beseechingly. Meaghan bit her lip over a smile that threatened to tip her from light-headed joy straight into happy tears.

"Hello," she whispered, patting the hellhound's nose. "Are you two better friends now?"

The hellhound huffed out a mouthful of smoke and wagged its tail. Meaghan laughed. "Okay. Let's go."

She swung herself up on the hound's back. Its muscles bunched and it leapt into the air. Meaghan whooped as the wind whipped past her face. The hellhound bounded across the snow, its paws crunching on snow and stepping lightly on thin air.

Meaghan laughed. The hellhound's joy was infectious. Its love for speeding through the night, with the sky full of stars above and the pristine snow below just waiting to be jumped on, sizzled through her golden mate-bond.

The snowy slopes gave way to white-sheeted pines. The hellhound slipped between them like a ghost, gleefully not leaving even a single broken twig as a trace of its passage. Meaghan laughed again.

"Show-off."

The hellhound woofed happily and Meaghan buried her face in the thick ruff of hair around its neck. *I don't think I've ever been this happy.* The shining light inside her glowed stronger, illuminating the thread that bound her to Caine more closely and intimately than she'd ever imagined could be possible.

They burst out of the trees into the clearing where Caine's cottage sat, snug and welcoming with warm light pouring from the windows. The hellhound crunched down into the snow on the front drive and waited patiently for Meaghan to slide off its back. Then it shook itself, shimmering, and Caine's arms were around her.

She stared up at him, and couldn't stop a bubble of laughter hiccupping out of her.

"What's so funny?" Caine squeezed her closer and kissed her forehead.

Meaghan nuzzled into Caine's naked shoulder. His body was hot beneath her hands, his pulse strong as she kissed his neck. Her own shoulders were shaking and she could barely speak around her giggles.

"You... you forgot your keys again..."

CHAPTER TWENTY-FIVE

Caine

Caine smacked his palm against his forehead. "Of all the—damn it." He looked up at the cottage. "I'll check the balcony door again. One minute…"

What are you doing? His hellhound nosed at him curiously. Caine silently explained about keys.

His hellhound huffed. *We don't need that. Just walk in. Like this.* It gave him a mental nudge and Caine stepped forward. *Like when I hid us from the alpha in the square, remember? You thought you were hiding under the trees. I was hiding us in the tree.* It bared its teeth in a wolfish laugh. *From the* ex *alpha.*

Caine reached out to the door. To his amazement, his hand passed straight through it.

"Holy…" He looked back over his shoulder at Meaghan. "One minute."

"Hey, I happen to know how long your 'one minutes' are—"

Caine held his breath and darted through the door. It was like walking through mist.

When he was on the other side he let out his breath in a rush. *All right, Hellhound. Now, let's not* do that again *while I open the door...*

The lock was solid under his hand. He unlocked the door and pulled it open. Meaghan's mouth was still open mid-sentence.

"Wow," she said.

"I can see that coming in useful," Caine reflected. His hellhound grumbled something and he frowned. It hadn't been words—more of a feeling. The same feelings he'd spent the whole year trying to force down. He frowned.

"What is it?"

"My hellhound. It's telling me that it's important that I use these abilities in the right way. To *do* right, not to do wrong, like Angus made the other hellhounds do." He paused. "I know that breaking into my own house isn't exactly chasing down evildoers, but I think it'll let me off the hook this time."

His hellhound huffed out a smoky laugh. *Breaking into your own den!*

"Do you want to talk about what happened?" Meaghan's voice was tentative. "I know you didn't want to go into it back at the Heartwells', and I don't want to push you into baring your heart, but..."

"I'll always bare my heart to you, Meaghan. Don't worry about that, not ever." Caine pulled her close and kissed her. "I told you my family was never really there for me growing up. Angus was. He was always getting into trouble, too, but I always assumed he was good at heart. I guess I let the fact that he was my friend blind me to who he really was."

Meaghan still looked concerned. Caine kissed her until the line disappeared from between her eyebrows.

"He's not going to hurt anyone else. Jackson put him and the other hellhounds away, and I don't know why, but I know they're not going to try anything."

"Even though they can walk through walls?"

They're not going to walk through anything, Caine's hellhound said smugly. *Not without permission.*

"We can forget about them for now," Caine told her. "Besides, I have other things on my mind."

He kissed her again, long and slow, and Meaghan smiled against his lips.

"Good," she murmured. "Me too."

The house was warmer than it had been the first time he brought Meaghan back here. Warmer and tidier and more like *home*. It gave Caine a sense of satisfaction that he recognized as coming from his hellhound.

A proper welcome for our mate, it said, flicking its ears. *Good.*

The temperature might have been more bearable, but Caine and Meaghan hurried upstairs as though they were being chased by icy winds. Meaghan was holding his hand tight as they ran together, but something was missing, he was sure of it; then they were in the bedroom, tumbling onto the bed, and Caine couldn't think of anything except how lucky he was.

Meaghan rolled onto her back beneath him. Her hands roved down his chest, leaving trails of fire across his skin. Caine moaned and she bit her lip over a delighted grin.

"This doesn't seem fair," she said. "You always ending up with no clothes on, while I'm all bundled up."

Caine brushed his fingertips along the edge of her jacket collar. "It's not fair at all."

He undid her coat button by button. When Meaghan raised herself up to pull it off, he gently moved her around until he was lying back and she was straddling him. The feeling of her weight on him made him groan with need.

"You're right," he said, his voice gravelly with need. "This isn't fair. I want to see and touch every inch of you."

Meaghan's eyes gleamed. Slowly—so slowly it made frustration thrum across every inch of his skin—she pulled her sweater over her head, revealing a t-shirt that hung loosely over her curves.

She took a deep breath. "What you're saying is, I shouldn't ask you to close your eyes this time?"

"Hell no." He grinned wickedly at her. "And I recall that being an *order*, not *asking*."

Her eyes creased with a grin she didn't bother biting back. Her smile stretched across her face, giddily free. "Oh, you want me to order you, huh? In the bedroom?"

"I wanted you to order me before. With Angus. I wanted you to command me not to obey him. But you did so much more than that." He cupped her face in his hands. "You weren't scared of my hellhound. You didn't need to command it to do the right thing, or chain it up. You trusted that we could win, together, and we did."

"Oh, Caine." Meaghan put her hands over his. "My love. I'd never chain you."

Except in the bedroom?

Her eyes widened. "Hey! You hush."

Caine mimed zipping his mouth shut and she groaned.

"You hush… if you want to."

"I don't. I want to tell you how much I love you. All the time." He slid his hands down her sides, then up under the hem of her shirt. "And how much I wish you'd hurry up and take this off."

She took off her t-shirt. Caine's cock throbbed at the way her body moved. Her wide hips and soft belly rocked slightly as she pulled the shirt over her head. He knew how she moved when she was lost in ecstasy. This tiny movement was a taste, a reminder, that made him even hungrier for more.

She reached one hand behind her back and undid her bra. One strap slipped off her shoulder, then the other, and she dropped her bra on the bed.

"Oh God." Caine sat up, holding her on his lap, and caressed her breasts. He ran his thumb over one of her nipples and she gasped. "You're incredible."

She made a soft noise at the back of her throat and Caine's hips jerked forward automatically. His cock was pressed up against Meaghan's belly, hard with need.

"You are," she replied, her voice breathy. "You're... *ahh.* Amazing."

Caine's hand slid down her back. Meaghan's hands were wandering too, her touch whipping his desire white hot.

Then her fingertips brushed up against the scar on his leg.

Meaghan's eyelashes whispered against his cheek. "Sorry." She drew her hand back, but Caine stopped her. He pressed her palm against the scar that punctured his thigh.

"That's how I got my hellhound," he murmured.

Meaghan's fingers tightened over the gnarled toothmarks. "Last time—"

The last time you touched my scar, I stopped you, and pulled away, and the next morning I acted like I couldn't wait to see the back of you. Caine dropped his head on her shoulder.

"Last time I was scared. I didn't know who or what I was. I do now." He pressed his lips against her shoulder, her neck, her lips that tasted like *home.* "I'm yours."

CHAPTER TWENTY-SIX

Meaghan

Meaghan's breath caught. "I love you."

She took his face in her hands and pushed him down until she was lying on top of him. Any worries she had about being too heavy, too clumsy, were swept away by Caine's groan of need.

"And I'm yours," she gasped as his hand slipped under the waistband of her pants to cup her backside. She raised her hips to undo her pants and wriggle out of them, and the back of her hand brushed against Caine's cock.

He jerked like he'd been hit by lightning.

Oh, shit. Meaghan swore out loud.

"What's wrong?"

She groaned and pounded one fist against the mattress. "Déjà vu. Same as last time. You don't have a key, and I don't have…"

She stopped.

"I love you," she whispered. "Every bit of you. I want to be with you, forever, and I should feel terrified saying that. But I don't. I'm not scared at all. And… I have something for you."

Before Caine could say anything, she jumped off the bed and found her jacket. She searched through the pockets. *It's here somewhere—aha!*

She climbed back into bed beside Caine and held out her closed hand.

He sat up. "What's this?"

"Your Christmas present."

His face fell. "I don't have anything for you—"

"Really? Nothing at all?" Meaghan teased. "When I went to all the trouble of kidnapping you." She grabbed his shoulders. "And shoving you in the dog-box." She pushed him down the mattress and straddled him. "And dragging you into town in your pajamas."

She rested her hands on his chest, feeling the strong beat of his heart. "And worst of all. When you were hurting, and beaten down, and thought you were a monster, I ran away. I left you."

Caine closed his hands over hers. "I drove you away."

"And I *let* you. You think people haven't tried to drive me away before? I'm the most annoying person I know. I pride myself on ignoring every hint short of a boot in the ass." She sighed. "I let you down."

Caine squeezed her hands. "You know that's not true. And even if it was—" Meaghan opened her mouth to argue and he pressed a finger over her lips. "It's over. There's no way things could have worked out that would make me happier than I am now."

"I know." Meaghan held her closed hand up so he could see it. "That's why this is for you."

Caine uncurled her fingers one by one and picked up the many-folded printout. "What's this?"

"My bus ticket. I was going to leave Pine Valley tomorrow. I thought there were only two ways this thing between us could end, and they both meant I had to leave."

"But you belong here."

"I do now." She wrapped his hands around the ticket. "So this is for you. A Christmas present from me, to tell you that I'm not going anywhere. You get all of me. And in return… I want all of you."

The surge of pure love and protectiveness that washed through their connection made her gasp. Caine's eyes burned.

He pulled her down and kissed her. Meaghan's body slid against his, hot and trembling.

"I love you," she murmured against his skin. His fingers tightened around her waist and the hot desire threading through Meaghan's veins tightened into anticipation. "I want you so much. More than anything. More than should actually be possible."

Caine rolled on top of her. "More than I deserve." The head of his cock pressed against Meaghan's entrance. She licked her lips.

"We just fought a pack of hellhounds and saved Christmas," she reminded him. "If you think you don't deserve—uh-h-h…"

Caine slid into her, so slowly her eyes flickered shut. The sensation was too much. He was thick, and hard, and *perfect*.

He held her close as he buried himself deep, their bodies fitting together like they were meant to be.

"We belong together," she breathed.

Caine swore softly, his back muscles tensing. He moved above her, slowly, controlled. Meaghan savored every moment. She'd never made love like this before. Caine was gentle, and loving, and…

The golden light inside her flared. Caine gasped and thrust harder. Pleasure tightened inside her and she wrapped her legs more tightly around his waist. His muscles were hard under her hands, his cock hitting every sensitive nerve inside her, sensation building until it was almost painful.

Meaghan's back arched as ecstasy rocked her body. She cried out. Caine kissed her, hard, and she buried her hands in his hair as tides of exquisite pleasure rolled over her, again and again.

Caine grabbed her hip and drove into her one last time. His whole body went tense, then he gave a throaty groan and Meaghan's body responded, pleasure surging against as he came inside her.

They lay there, wrapped together. Meaghan's body was heavy with satisfaction. She closed her eyes.

"Did you feel that?" Caine panted.

Eyes still closed, Meaghan raised her eyebrows.

"Not… damn it," Caine said. He placed his hand on her chest, spreading his fingers wide. "There. The light inside. It's brighter now."

Meaghan held her breath. The tiny sun felt like it was less than an inch beneath his palm. She concentrated, searching for the threads that she'd sensed before, connecting her to Caine.

"The connection," she murmured. "The one that lets us talk to each other…" *…like this.*

Our mate-bond.

Caine pushed himself up on his elbows and gazed down at her. Sparks kindled in his night-sky eyes.

"My hellhound has been protecting it ever since we met. It was tiny then. Barely as big as a match flame."

"I thought I was imagining it." Meaghan rested her hand on his chest. "Thank God for your hellhound. What if it had gone out?"

"It didn't. My hellhound was keeping it safe. For this. This… second chance. A new beginning."

Warmth blossomed from the tiny sun in Meaghan's heart, filling her body.

"The beginning of something amazing," she said.

EPILOGUE

Caine

CHRISTMAS MORNING

Meaghan was asleep. And she was gorgeous asleep—incredible, beautiful, so stunning he could have watched her all day—but there was no way he was letting this opportunity go to waste.

We have to feed our mate, his hellhound insisted.

That's what I'm doing! he retorted. *What do you think this looks like?*

It looks like that mud water you drank when you were sad, his hellhound replied. *And small hard balls.*

"They're *eggs*," Caine said out loud, exasperated. "Watch."

He cracked one into a bowl. His hellhound watched carefully. It wasn't impressed.

"You cook them with butter, and salt and pepper. She'll like them. I promise."

I hope you're right.

"And there's cream for the coffee."

Mud water.

"Look, do you want me to finish this before she wakes up, or do you want to keep complaining?"

Something fluttered outside the kitchen window and Caine raised his head. His hellhound went still, all its senses alert.

Someone's out there.

I can't smell them from in here, his hellhound complained.

He reached over the counter and opened the kitchen window. A shadow passed over him, and then something small and papery landed on his nose.

"Hey!" Caine caught the card before it fell in the eggs. "What—"

He peered at the card. "This is the Christmas card I sent from the Sweetheart Track at the Puppy Express."

Caine leaned out the window and caught a glimpse of feathery white wings swooping away.

Olly? he called out. *I thought these were meant to go out on Christmas Eve?*

Olly's voice buzzed into his head, along with a strong sensation that she wanted to peck him. *Do you know how long it takes to fly out here? Live closer to town next year if you want your deliveries on time!*

Caine chuckled and put the scrambled eggs on the heat. Eggs and coffee… his hellhound might have a point. It wasn't much of a Christmas morning breakfast.

He'd have to make it up to her. Preferably in a way that would make their mate-bond glow even more.

*

Fortunately—or unfortunately—Meaghan's eyes lit up when she saw him carrying in the breakfast platter.

223

"Oh my God," she moaned. "Eggs? Coffee? You're a mira-cle-worker. Bread? This is amazing." She took a bite and chewed with her eyes shut, which was so distracting Caine forgot all about his own food. "We never even had dinner last night, what with… everything. No wonder I'm starving. And coffee!"

She likes the sad mud water? Caine's hellhound was confused.

Lots of humans do. Caine ate his own breakfast slowly, mostly enjoying watch Meaghan eat.

"What do you want for Christmas dinner?" he asked when they were finished.

Meaghan's eyes lit up. "No one has ever asked me that before." She hugged her knees to her chest. "What are the options?"

"Er… eggs and coffee?"

"What happened to all the leftovers Mrs. Holborn gave you? Don't tell me you ate them all!"

"I had a broken heart to feed." Caine laid one hand on his chest, sighing dramatically.

She laughed and threw a pillow at him. "Tease!"

"Tease?" He knocked the pillow away and crawled over the bed towards her. "That's not teasing. *This* is teasing…"

He grabbed her ankle and kissed it, then trailed his lips up her leg, feeling her tremble as he got further and further up.

Human, his hellhound whispered, *there's something you should know.*

Not now, Hellhound, Caine muttered back.

I have a Christmas present for you both, too.

Caine paused as his hellhound waved its tail sheepishly. Suspicion made him narrow his eyes.

"God, you *are* a tease," Meaghan breathed, blinking heavy-lidded eyes at him. "Wait. Is something wrong?"

"My hellhound's telling me it got us a Christmas present."

Meaghan touched her chest. "And you're worried? I thought you trusted it now."

"I would, if it wasn't acting like a puppy that doesn't want you to look at what it did to your shoes," Caine explained.

The doorbell rang.

Here's your present!

Caine cocked an eyebrow at Meaghan. "He says that's the present now."

"Now I'm worried, too." Meaghan rolled off the bed and pulled on her clothes. Caine followed suit.

Can you sense anything about what's out there? she asked as he padded down the stairs in front of her.

No. Nothing.

"Oh. *Oh.* I wonder…"

Caine pulled the door open. Three young men were standing behind it, looking as sheepish as his hellhound felt. They were a ragtag bunch, exhausted-looking and somehow familiar.

Caine frowned. "Who are you?"

Two of the young men elbowed the other one forward. He ducked his head. "We're, um. We're your pack," he explained to his feet. "You defeated Mr. Parker, so that makes you the new alpha."

Merry Christmas! Caine's hellhound barked. Behind him, Meaghan stifled a bubble of laughter.

Caine gulped. *Life in Pine Valley is going to be more complicated than I thought…*

A NOTE FROM ZOE CHANT

Thank you for buying my book! I hope you enjoyed it.

If you'd like to be emailed when I release my next book, please visit www.zoechant.com/join-my-mailing-list/ to be added to my mailing list. You can also follow me on Facebook or Twitter!

Please consider reviewing *Christmas Hellhound*, even if you only write a line or two. I appreciate all reviews, whether positive or negative.

CPSIA information can be obtained
at www.ICGtesting.com
Printed in the USA
LVHW100025090123
736730LV00001B/78